MINDWORK
PUBLISHING COMPANY
presents

SHATTERED VOWS

This is a work of fiction. Names, characters, businesses, places, events, and incidents are either the product of the authors' imagination or used in a fictitious manner. Any resemblance to actual persons, living or dead, or actual events is purely coincidental.

This book is intended for entertainment and reflection. It is not a substitute for professional mental health advice, diagnosis, or treatment. Readers seeking support should consult a qualified therapist or counselor.

Mindwork Publishing LLC

254 Chapman Rd, Ste 208 #22316

Newark, Delaware 19702

CONTENTS

1. HOLLOW PERFECTION 1

2. INVISIBLE WOUNDS 20

3. REKINDLED 48

4. FAULT LINES 66

5. CROSSED BOUNDARIES 90

6. PRECIPICE 114

7. CONFRONTATION 136

8. EXCAVATION 160

9. LANDMINES 187

10. TESTING GROUNDS 213

11. RECONSTRUCTION 240

12. RENEWED VOWS 267

Chapter One

Hollow Perfection

Kareem Campbell adjusted the lilies and hydrangeas in the centerpiece, his practiced fingers working with the precise attention to detail that had earned him steady promotions at the investment firm where he'd worked for the past nine years. Everything had to be perfect tonight. He stepped back, surveying the dining room with a critical eye: the good china they'd received as wedding gifts laid out precisely, sterling silver flatware polished to a mirror shine, crystal wine glasses positioned just so. The unlit candles waited patiently, like actors before their cue, and a bottle of cabernet from their Napa honeymoon trip stood breathing—a wine he'd been saving for a special occasion.

Seven years.

The phrase echoed in his mind as he checked his watch—6:45 PM. Fallon had texted that she'd be home by 7:00, which meant 7:30 if the Henderson merger was as complicated as she'd mentioned in her brief morning conversation. Her text had been characteristically efficient: *Late meeting. Home by 7. Don't wait on dinner.* But he would wait, of course. That's what he always did. The salmon would be flawless, the asparagus tender-crisp, the potatoes golden and fragrant with rosemary. He'd made her favorite dessert too—dark chocolate mousse with a hint of orange—though he couldn't remember the last time he'd actually seen her indulge in dessert. Lately, she'd been passing on anything that wasn't "productive" to her body or career, another casualty of her partnership track. His phone buzzed on the counter. Devon.

You all set for the big anniversary? Knock her socks off, man.

Kareem smiled faintly, typing back: *Table's set. Food's almost ready. Just need the wife to show up.*

Devon's response was immediate: *She better. Some of us would kill for what you got. Solid marriage, nice house, no drama. Vanessa's been on my ass all week about some family thing this weekend.*

Kareem's thumb hovered over the screen. Devon didn't know about the growing hollowness, the polite conversations that never went deeper than weather and work schedules. Devon always said they had it made—the house, the cars, the Christmas cards with their practiced smiles. Even their arguments were quiet, civilized affairs, nothing like the passionate fights Devon described having with Vanessa. He set the phone down without responding. Last month she'd worked through his surprise dinner. Last week she'd rescheduled their planned Saturday morning coffee. Small erasures, each one reasonable on its own. The timer on the oven beeped, pulling him back to the task at hand. The salmon was done—timed exactly for a 7:00 arrival. He'd keep it warm, as he'd learned to do over the years. Just in case.

Kareem moved efficiently around the kitchen, his movements as precise as they were in every aspect of his life. Control was comfortable. Control was safe. The spreadsheets at work, the carefully balanced investment portfolios, the meticulous meal planning—all of it provided structure he could rely on when other things felt increasingly uncertain. He adjusted the salmon's position on the plate—the same precision that had earned Davis's rare nod of approval this week. "Good attention to detail, Campbell." At work, the rules made sense. Marriage, he was discovering, operated under murkier principles. The effort-reward relationship wasn't nearly so linear. He'd tried being more attentive—planning date nights, bringing home small gifts, sending thoughtful texts during the day. He'd tried giving her space—handling more household tasks without being asked, not questioning her increasingly late nights at the office. He'd tried everything except the one thing that terrified him most: directly confronting the growing distance between them. Because what if she simply didn't care anymore? What if asking the question only forced her to articulate an answer he wasn't prepared to hear? Kareem glanced at his watch again: 7:15. No additional text, which could mean she was driving or simply hadn't bothered to update him. He lit the candles and poured himself a small glass of wine, just enough to take the edge off the anticipation that was gradually morphing into disappointment.

At 7:42, Kareem heard the garage door open. He quickly relit the candles that had burned down considerably and straightened his button-down shirt—dark blue, her favorite. The food was plated and waiting under warming lids, his own culinary sleight of hand to maintain the illusion of perfect timing. He heard her heels click across the hardwood in the foyer, followed by the familiar thud of her briefcase being set down on the entryway bench. Her footsteps stopped. Started again, slower. Fallon appeared in the doorway, still in her tailored suit. Despite the late hour, she looked immaculate—her hair styled in a sophisticated updo, gold drop earrings catching the candlelight. The controlled exterior that served her so well in courtrooms and boardrooms. Her eyes—sharp, intelligent, perpetually evaluating—scanned the setup strategically before recognition flickered across her face. For just a moment, something that might have been guilt crossed her features before the courtroom attorney returned

"Oh," she said simply. "I forgot what day it was."

The admission stung more than if she'd said nothing at all. Kareem felt the familiar tightening in his chest—the sensation that had become his constant companion in their marriage.

“Really? Well, that’s understandable. Between mergers and acquisitions, who has time to remember little things like anniversaries? I mean, it's only seven years of unparalleled devotion."

Fallon nods, her tone neutral and almost dismissive. "Right," she says, as if acknowledging a trivial calendar appointment. "Let me just change first."

Kareem nodded, his tone light but edged with sarcasm. "Sure. I’ll just keep the food warm—" he mumbled the rest, "like I’ve been keeping this relationship. No rush."

Fallon hesitated, her eyes darting from the table to the stairs. Something shifted in her expression. It was the same look she got when clients called during dinner. "Give me two minutes to wash up."

As she disappeared upstairs, Kareem took a larger sip of wine than he'd intended. Seven years. Seven years, and she'd forgotten. Not misremembered—forgotten entirely. He wondered if their anniversary was even in her meticulously maintained digital calendar, or if it had been crowded out by depositions and client meetings and partnership track milestones. Four minutes later, Fallon returned, having removed her suit jacket but otherwise unchanged. No special effort. Not even a different pair of earrings. She'd washed her hands and face, reapplied her lipstick, and apparently decided that was sufficient acknowledgment of the occasion. They sat across from each other, the candles casting shadows across Fallon's face as she cut her salmon into perfect bites. The silence stretched between them, neither comfortable nor entirely uncomfortable—just familiar. This was their new normal: existing in the same space without truly being together.

"This is good," she said after a calculated silence.

"Thanks." Kareem took another sip of wine, searching for something to fill the space between them. "How was your day?"

"Henderson's CFO is renegotiating." Her words came out sharp, clipped. "Months of work down the drain because he can't handle being outmaneuvered by a woman."

Kareem nodded, recognizing her deflection strategy—intellectual discussion to avoid personal connection. "You'll find a way to make it work. You always do."

"It's just business," Fallon said, dismissing his comment with a small wave of her fork. "Either they'll come around, or we'll walk away. That's the leverage." She finally looked up from her plate, her professional mask slipping just enough to reveal the exhaustion underneath. There was something else there too—a flicker of what might have been longing, quickly banished—as she asked, "How was your day?"

"Pretty good, actually," Kareem said, latching onto the small opening, desperate for real conversation. "Got the quarterly projections finished early. Davis actually said 'good work,' which from him is basically like witnessing the second coming." He smiled, hoping for a moment of shared humor.

Fallon's lips curved slightly, but the smile didn't reach her eyes. "That's good."

"Yeah, I think we're on track to exceed targets this quarter. The tech sector is outperforming our projections, and the new sustainable energy fund is..." He stopped himself, recognizing he was now the one hiding behind work talk. "Anyway, it was a good day."

The conversation lapsed into silence again. Kareem cut into his salmon, which had cooled considerably despite his best efforts. He tried to remember when they'd last had a conversation that went deeper than surface exchanges of information. When had Fallon last asked him how he felt about something, rather than just what he thought? When had he last done the same for her? Across the table, Fallon's fork paused midway to her mouth. She seemed lost in thought, her gaze focused on something distant. For just a moment, the carefully constructed attorney vanished, replaced by a woman carrying some invisible weight. She caught herself quickly, straightening her posture and resuming her meal with mechanical precision.

"Did you hear about the Johnsons?" he asked finally. "They're getting divorced."

Fallon raised an eyebrow, suddenly more interested. "Stephanie and Allen? From the block party last summer?"

"Yeah. Allen moved out last weekend. Dave next door said there was a moving truck on Sunday."

"Hmm." Fallon took a measured sip of wine, her analytical mind visibly processing the information. "She should have seen it coming."

The coldness in her voice startled him, though it shouldn't have. "What do you mean?"

Fallon's fork paused midair. "She kept grabbing his arm at that party." A small, cold smile. "Desperate."

Something in Kareem's chest tightened. Was that how she saw their marriage too? Was he the one desperately trying to connect while she was already checked out?

"Maybe they're going through a rough patch," he offered, as much to himself as to her. "Not every marriage is perfect all the time."

Fallon's eyes met his, something unreadable in them. She opened her mouth as if to say one thing, then closed it, opting instead for the safer legal perspective. "Rough patches don't lead to moving vans,

Kareem. By the time someone moves out, it's been over for years." She placed her napkin beside her plate with precise movements. "I see it every day at the firm. People finally admitting what they've known all along but were too afraid to say."

The word "years" hung in the air between them.

"I got you something," Kareem said, changing the subject, reaching under the table for the small wrapped box he'd hidden there earlier.

Fallon looked at it for a moment before carefully unwrapping it, her movements methodical and controlled. Inside was a silver pendant necklace with their initials intertwined—the kind of sentimental gift he knew she wouldn't have chosen for herself but that he hoped might remind her of what they once had.She held the necklace up to the light, her fingers tracing the initials. "K and F." A pause.

"It's beautiful."

"You're welcome." He waited, the silence stretching between them.

For a moment, their eyes met across the candlelit table. Fallon's hand started toward his, paused mid-way, then withdrew as she busied herself with her napkin. Something flickered across her face—regret, perhaps, or the quiet realization of what she was letting slip away. She had once confessed, early in their marriage, "It's not that I don't care—I just don't know how to be any different." Kareem wished she'd say something like that now—anything to show him the woman he'd fallen in love with was still reachable. Instead, Fallon checked her watch.

"I need to review some files before tomorrow. I've got an early meeting with the partners."

And just like that, the wall was back up, higher than before.

"Yeah, sure," Kareem said, the familiar disappointment settling like sediment in his stomach. "I'll clean up."

Fallon stood, hesitating for a moment like she might say something else. She glanced at the candles, at the remnants of the meal he'd prepared, and for a split second, conflict played across her face—as if part of her recognized what she was walking away from but couldn't figure out how to stay. Instead, she just picked up the necklace box. "Thank you." Her fingers lingered on the box. "For all of this." Kareem watched

Fallon walk away, her posture perfectly straight, even in their empty house where there was no one to impress. As she headed upstairs, he shook his head and muttered to himself, "Seven years, and I'm competing with PowerPoint presentations and partnership tracks. Maybe I should draft a proposal for quality time—make it sound like a corporate merger. She might actually prioritize it."

After cleaning up dishes that could have gone in the dishwasher but gave his restless hands something to do, Kareem poured himself another glass of wine and wandered into the living room. Photos from happier times lined the built-in shelves—their wedding, where Fallon's elegant hair had been adorned with pearls that matched her gown, a trip to Jamaica three years ago, a charity gala where they'd both received community leadership awards. He picked up a silver frame containing a photo from their second anniversary. They'd gone to a bed and breakfast in Vermont, spent the weekend hiking and drinking local wine.

In the picture, Fallon was laughing—really laughing, head thrown back, eyes crinkled at the corners—as he kissed her cheek. He couldn't remember what he'd said to make her laugh like that, but he remembered how it felt. Like winning something precious. Like being exactly where he was supposed to be. When was the last time he'd heard her really laugh? The kind that came from deep in her belly, unrestrained and genuine? He couldn't remember. Kareem set the photo down carefully and moved to the French doors leading to their back patio. Outside, the late spring air was cool but not unpleasant. Their backyard was as meticulously maintained as everything else in their lives—landscaped beds of perennials that would bloom in carefully planned succession throughout the summer, a stone patio with high-end furniture, subtle landscape lighting illuminating paths and accent plants. They'd designed it together, back when "together" still meant something more than occupying the same spaces at different times. Fallon had surprised him then with her knowledge of plants—a hobby her grandmother had instilled in her that she rarely mentioned anymore. She'd sketched out planting schemes, researched bloom times, insisted on native species that would support local pollinators. That passion seemed as foreign now as the sound of her genuine laughter. Somewhere along the way, Fallon had filed away these softer parts of herself, these interests that weren't directly applicable to her career advancement. Or perhaps she'd simply stopped sharing them with him. His phone buzzed in his pocket. Devon again:

How'd it go? She love it?

Kareem stared at the screen, unsure how to explain the complicated emptiness he felt. Finally, he typed:

Anniversary went... as expected. Let's just say the salmon had more warmth than the atmosphere. I could use a reality check."

He put his phone away and looked up at their bedroom window. The light was still on, but he knew Fallon wouldn't be waiting for him. She'd be propped up against her pillows, reading briefs or case files, her reading glasses perched on her nose, her mind already in tomorrow's meetings. At what point did a marriage become just a house-sharing arrangement? At what point did two people who had promised to love and cherish each other become roommates with occasional benefits and shared financial responsibilities? His phone buzzed again. He pulled it out, expecting another text from Devon, but it was Fallon:

Going to bed. Early start tomorrow. Don't forget to set the alarm.

She'd almost written something else—he could tell from the typing indicator that had appeared, disappeared, and reappeared before this final message arrived. No mention of their anniversary. No acknowledgment of his efforts. Just logistics and reminders, as if he were another item on her to-do list. Kareem drained his wine glass and went back inside, locking the French doors behind him. He moved through the house on autopilot, turning off lights, checking that the front door was locked, setting the alarm system. Routines were comforting. Routines made sense when other things didn't. Upstairs, the bedroom was dark, Fallon already asleep—or pretending to be. Her breathing was too measured, too controlled for genuine sleep, but he didn't challenge the pretense. It was easier this way. No awkward navigation of whether they should touch, whether sex was expected on an anniversary they clearly viewed very differently. He undressed quietly in the dark and slipped into his side of the bed, careful to stay on his designated half. The mattress might as well have been two separate beds for all the contact they had these days.

"Goodnight," he said softly, not expecting a response.

He didn't get one, though he thought he felt her body tense slightly at the sound of his voice, as if she too was aware of the distance between them but didn't know how to cross it.

His phone buzzed on the nightstand. Devon:

Forgot to say happy anniversary earlier. Hope you got some tonight, man. You deserve it after putting up with lawyer hours all these years.

Kareem almost laughed at how wide of the mark Devon's assumption was. Sex had become as scheduled and efficient as everything else in their lives, usually initiated by him, sometimes agreed to by her if she wasn't too tired. Never spontaneous, never passionate. Just another box to check. Kareem stared at the text for a moment, then typed back:

She forgot it was our anniversary.

Devon's follow-up text came a moment later: *Drinks tomorrow? Sounds like you need a friend who actually remembers your anniversary.*

Kareem looked at the text, then over at Fallon's still form in the darkness. She'd removed her makeup, changed into silk pajamas, and was now facing away from him, her body curled slightly, protecting herself even in sleep. He rolled onto his back and stared at the ceiling, feeling a weight in his chest that seemed to grow heavier by the day. The weight of words unsaid, of questions unasked, of a loneliness that somehow felt more acute for being experienced right next to someone else. He pulled out his wallet and flipped it open, the dim light from the window illuminating the worn photo he still kept tucked inside—their wedding day. In the picture, Fallon wore an elegant white gown, her hair adorned with pearl pins, and her arms wrapped around his neck. Kareem stood tall in his black tuxedo, and they looked at each other like they were everything they'd ever wanted.

"I promise to choose you every day," she'd said in her vows. "To choose us, even when it's difficult."

When had she stopped choosing them? Or had he stopped first, in ways he hadn't recognized? Kareem traced his thumb over Fallon's face in the photo before tucking it away and picking up his phone. He typed a response to Devon:

Yeah. I think I do.

He set his phone back on the nightstand. Kareem lay awake listening for some sign—a sigh, a shift in breathing, anything that might tell him she was thinking about their anniversary too. But Fallon's side of the bed remained still, and eventually even the sound of her breathing faded into the white noise of their central air, leaving him alone with the echo of her "Oh" and the memory of her hand, stopping just short of his across the table.

Chapter Two

Invisible Wounds

The upscale restaurant buzzed with the midday rush of business lunches and clinking glasses. Kareem checked his watch—12:15—and scanned the room for Devon. The hostess had already shown him to their usual spot, a corner table tucked behind a decorative divider that gave a little bit of privacy. The scent of seared meat and expensive cologne hung in the air, mixing with the quiet buzz of business conversations.

Kareem traced his finger along the edge of the crisp, white napkin, feeling its slightly rough texture against his skin. His water glass was already sweating, little drops sliding down to the shiny wooden table.

"My man!" Devon's voice boomed from behind, drawing more attention than Kareem was comfortable with. Devon Shaw walked through the restaurant like he owned the place, moving with the kind of confidence that made people take notice. His sharp suit and big smile created an impression of success and energy.

Kareem stood to greet him with the elaborate handshake they'd perfected since college. "What's good? You're actually on time for once."

"Well now, you know I couldn't leave my boy hanging on a day like this!" Devon grinned, dropping into the chair across from him and signaling the waiter. "Anniversary aftermath calls for some serious brotherly support."

“Now how bad was it? She chuck the gift at your head or hit you with that ol’ frosty, arms-crossed, sleepin’-on-the-couch kind of cold shoulder?” Devon questioned.

Kareem hesitated. Devon was his oldest friend, the person who'd seen him through breakups, job changes, and the death of his father. But there was something about discussing his marriage troubles that felt like a betrayal—even if there was nothing left to betray.

"That bad, huh?" Devon raised an eyebrow. "Boy, look at you. You ain't even have to say anything. Your face got more drama than a daytime soap opera."

"She forgot," Kareem said finally, his words dripping with cultured indignation. "Completely forgot our anniversary. Can you imagine? Seven years of distinguished devotion, and she lets the date slip away."

Devon gave a slow, impressed shake of his head. "Forgot?! That's cold, man. Even for Fallon, that's ice cold. Forget your anniversary? See, that right there... that's disrespectful!"

"Yeah, well." Kareem shrugged, trying to project casual indifference. "It's just a date, right? No big deal. I mean, I'm not the type to stress over the small stuff."

"Man, stop." Devon leaned forward, his voice dropping. "Be real with yourself—'just a date'? That's thee date. The one you can't forget unless you try to sleep on the couch for the next three decades."

The waiter came over, and before Kareem could say a word, Devon took charge, ordering for both of them.

"Yeah, yeah, two steaks—medium rare. And don't be bringing no flimsy bread this time, alright?

The waiter, a bit startled, gave a quick nod and hurried away.

"Look here, man. Vanessa? That woman drives me up the wall sometimes. But let me tell you something—she'd never forget our anniversary. That's just basic respect."

Respect. The word settled in Kareem's mind, finally giving form to a feeling he'd never quite understood. Was that what was missing? Did Fallon no longer respect him? Or had she ever?

"Maybe she's just busy," Kareem offered weakly. "The Henderson merger is—"

"Ain't it always something?" Devon cut him off. "When do you become the priority?"

The question hung between them as their drinks arrived. Kareem took a long sip of water, buying time before answering.

"It's complicated," he said finally.

Devon's eyes narrowed. "No, it's not. You're making it complicated. Marriage works in different ways for different people." He leaned closer, lowering his voice. "Look here, me and Vanessa—we got ourselves an... arrangement."

"An arrangement," Kareem repeated, already knowing where this was going.

Devon shrugged, a slight smile playing at the corners of his mouth. "Sometimes you gotta call it what it is. Some of us? We get what we need... elsewhere." He carefully adjusted his cufflinks—gold with small diamonds, probably another gift from his latest "elsewhere."

Kareem shifted uncomfortably. Devon had been dropping hints about his infidelities for years, but never this explicitly. "Listen, Devon," Kareem said firmly. "Let's get one thing straight. I'm a man of principle. I don't sacrifice my values just for a moment of pleasure. That's not who I am."

"Listen here, man, nobody is built for emotional starvation. You keep acting like you supposed to just take it." Devon countered, leaning back as their steaks arrived. "Just food for thought. Speaking of which—" He gestured to their plates with an easy smile, pivoting away from the heaviness of the conversation. "Now come on, eat up! I'm not trying' to sit here while you philosophize on an empty stomach. You over here starving emotionally and physically. Get it together!"

Kareem welcomed the break. For a few minutes, they ate in easy silence—the kind that only comes from nearly twenty years of friendship.

"So," Devon said eventually, cutting into his steak with precise movements, "is that therapy still doing anything for you? Or are you just paying' somebody to listen to you whine?

Another topic Kareem had avoided discussing with Devon, who considered therapy "paying someone to tell you what your boys would say for free."

"It is, actually," Kareem admitted. "Dr. Harper possesses a certain... finesse in her craft."

"And Fallon still doesn't know?"

Kareem shook his head. "Hasn't asked where I go every Tuesday afternoon."

Devon's expression hardened slightly. "Hold up, hold up—so you mean to tell me she don't even notice you're gone?"

"I don't think it's that she doesn't notice," Kareem said carefully. "She just doesn't ask."

"Same difference." Devon speared a piece of steak with unnecessary force. "Look,man, I'm not trying to gang up on you, but let's cut the bull. You have to ask yourself—what are you really fighting' for, huh? The marriage... or just the fantasy of one? 'Cause right now, you sound like you more in love with the concept than the reality."

The question hit closer to home than Kareem wanted to admit. He checked his watch—1:20. "Ah shoot. I gotta go. Got a therapy appointment at two."

Devon nodded, the momentary tension dissolving. ""Yeah, yeah. Tell Dr. Feel-Good I said she is wasting her time." He grinned to soften the words. "You know what you need to do. You just don't want to admit it yet."

Dr. Adrienne Harper's office occupied the third floor of a converted Victorian in the old part of the city. The waiting room was deliberately calming—soft blues and greens, comfortable chairs, the gentle sound of a water feature in the corner. A faint scent of lavender hung in the air, and the thick carpet absorbed sound in a way that made the space feel insulated from the world outside. Kareem had grown to appreciate the tranquility of this space over the past four months of weekly sessions.

"Kareem," Dr. Harper appeared in the doorway, her warm smile crinkling the corners of her eyes behind round tortoiseshell glasses. Her locs, streaked with dignified gray, were pulled back in a loose style that somehow managed to look both professional and approachable. "Come on in."

He followed her into the familiar office, taking his usual seat in the leather armchair angled toward her desk.

"How are you today?" she asked, her voice carrying the calm assurance that had helped him open up during their first session.

"I'm okay," he said automatically, then caught himself. "Actually, no. Yesterday was our anniversary. Seven years."

Dr. Harper's expression remained neutral but attentive. "How did that go?"

Kareem let out a dry, mirthless chuckle. “Well, let’s just say it wasn’t exactly a champagne-popping, jazz-playing, slow-dance-under-the-stars kind of evening." He leaned back, crossing his legs. "She forgot."

"I see." Dr. Harper made a brief note. "And how did that make you feel?"

"Like I'm invisible," Kareem said, the words emerging before he could filter them. "No, actually—more like a ghost in a museum. There, but invisible. Drifting through the rooms of our home without anyone really seeing me, hearing me... or even reaching for me."

"That's a powerful image," Dr. Harper observed. "The ghost in your own house."

Kareem nodded, feeling the pressure building behind his eyes. He wouldn't cry here. He hadn't cried since his father's funeral five years ago. Men in his family didn't cry; they solved problems. But what if the problem couldn't be solved?

"I had lunch with Devon today," he said, changing the subject slightly.

"Your friend from college," Dr. Harper recalled. "The one who's having affairs."

"Yeah." Kareem shifted in his seat. "He thinks I should—"

“Before we talk about Devon’s perspective, I’d like to stay with that powerful image you just shared." Dr. Harper interrupted gently. "What do you think it says about how you see yourself in the relationship?"

The question hung in the air. What did he think? These were questions he'd gotten so used to not asking himself that they felt almost foreign.

"I think..." he began slowly, "I think I'm tired. Tired of investing the best of myself into someone who seems not to notice. Or care."

"How would you describe the emotional connection between you and Fallon earlier in your relationship compared to now? Were there particular qualities or moments that felt different?"

The question transported Kareem back—not to their early dating days when everything was new and exciting—but to a specific moment, about six months into their relationship.

They'd been at a party at Fallon's law school classmate's apartment. Kareem had stepped away to get drinks, returning to find Fallon deep in conversation with a professor she admired. He'd waited patiently at the edge of the group until Fallon noticed him and drew him in with a warm smile.

"This is Kareem," she'd said, her hand finding his, fingers intertwining. "He's the one I was telling you about, Professor Winters."

The older woman had smiled. "Ah, the financial whiz who's also apparently an excellent cook. Fallon says your risotto is life-changing."

Kareem had laughed, surprised and pleased that Fallon had talked about him, had shared details of their private life with someone she respected.

Later that night, curled together in her small apartment, he'd mentioned it.

"You told your professor about my risotto?"

Fallon had looked up at him, her eyes soft in a way they rarely were in public. "Of course I did. It is life-changing." Her hand had trailed along his jaw. "You're changing my life, Kareem Campbell. I didn't think I had room for someone else's dreams alongside mine, but somehow, you fit."

"She wasn't always like this," Kareem said finally. "When we first met, she was... guarded, yes. Careful. But once you got past those initial walls, there was such warmth there. Such passion." He looked down at his hands. "She used to tell me things. Important things, small things. She used to listen when I talked about my day, really listen. Sometimes she'd reference something I'd mentioned weeks before, and I'd be surprised she remembered."

"What changed?" Dr. Harper asked.

Kareem shook his head. "I don't know exactly. It was gradual. After we got married, it was like she. .. retreated, somehow. Started working later, talking less. Every conversation became about logistics—bills, schedules, household tasks."

"Did anything significant happen around that time? A loss, a career change, family issues?"

Kareem thought about it. "Her father called after our honeymoon. They'd been estranged for years, but suddenly he wanted to reconnect. Fallon was... different after that. Harder somehow."

Dr. Harper made another note. "Tell me about Fallon's parents."

"Fallon's parents divorced when she was twelve," Kareem said. "It was messy, but honestly, she doesn't talk about it much. Just bits and pieces over the years." He paused, realizing how little he actually knew about that formative period in her life. "Her father left for another woman. Her mother took it hard, that's all I really know."

"And you think this shaped how Fallon approaches relationships?"

Kareem shrugged. "I guess? I mean, it would make sense, right? But whenever I try to dig deeper, she changes the subject." He ran a hand over his close-cropped hair. "It's like hitting a wall."

"So you've constructed a narrative to explain her behavior," Dr. Harper observed.

"What do you mean?"

"You're filling in gaps with assumptions. It's natural—humans seek patterns and explanations. But I'm curious about what Fallon herself has actually shared about how she views intimacy and vulnerability."

Kareem considered the question. "Not much, to be honest. She keeps that part of herself locked away." He stared at his hands. "Sometimes I think I'm married to a stranger."

"So how do you feel in the relationship?"

Kareem laughed bitterly. "Like I'm being tested somehow. Like there's this impossible standard I can never meet." He searched for the right words. "It's almost like... like she's daring me to either accept the emptiness or be the one who gives up."

Dr. Harper tilted her head slightly. "That's an interesting description. When you say 'dare,' what do you mean exactly?"

"I don't know," Kareem admitted, the certainty he'd felt a moment ago slipping away. "Sometimes it feels like she's waiting for me to fail some test I didn't know I was taking." He shook his head. "But that doesn't make sense, does it? Why would she want our marriage to fail?"

"I'm not suggesting she wants that," Dr. Harper said carefully. "But sometimes our past experiences create patterns we're not even aware of."

Kareem let that sit for a moment, her words settling somewhere just beneath the surface.

"When we first started dating," Kareem said, changing direction, "there were moments where I felt like I really knew her, you know? Not just the lawyer, but the person underneath."

"What changed, in your view?"

"I wish I knew," Kareem said, genuine confusion in his voice. "After we got married, something shifted. Maybe the pressure of making partner? Her father tried to reconnect around that time too, which seemed to shake her up."

Dr. Harper made a note. "Did she share how she felt about that contact from her father?"

"Not really. Just said he wanted to 'play family' now that it was convenient for him." Kareem frowned, remembering. "She took the call, but I don't think they've spoken since. She never explained exactly what happened, and I... I guess I didn't push."

"Tell me about the decision not to have children," Dr. Harper said. "Was that mutual?"

The question caught Kareem off guard. "We always said we'd wait until her career was more established.

Then it became about buying the house, then her making partner..." He trailed off. "I guess we never really had a direct conversation about changing the plan. It just... shifted."

"And how do you feel about that?"

"I don't know," Kareem admitted. "Sometimes I think a child would force us to communicate better, to be more present. Other times I'm relieved we don't have that complication."

"That's understandable." Dr. Harper wrote in her notes. "Now, last session, we talked about your tendency to avoid conflict, particularly with Fallon. You mentioned that you haven't told her you're coming to therapy. Can we explore that a bit more today?"

Kareem nodded reluctantly. This was the part of therapy he found most challenging—examining his own contribution to the problems in his marriage.

"I guess I don't tell her because..." he paused, searching for honesty. "Because then I'd have to tell her why I'm here. And that would mean confronting her with how unhappy I am."

"And what do you imagine would happen if you did that?"

"Best case? She'd intellectualize it. Turn it into a problem to solve, like one of her cases." He sighed. "Worst case? She'd shut down completely. Maybe even leave."

"Are you sure about that? That she'd leave?"

Kareem considered the question. "No," he admitted. "Actually, I think I'm more afraid she wouldn't leave. That she'd just... accept it. Like, 'Yes, we're miserable, but that's marriage, Kareem. Grow up.'"

Dr. Harper nodded. "So perhaps the fear isn't about her reaction, but about confirmation. Confirmation that she knows about your unhappiness and isn't motivated to change."

"Yeah," Kareem said softly. "Because then what? Then I have to make a choice."

"What kind of choice?"

"Whether to stay like this forever or... not." Kareem couldn't bring himself to say the word "leave." Not yet.

Dr. Harper let the silence stretch for a moment, giving weight to his words. "Kareem, I'd like to ask you something." She set her notebook aside, leaning forward slightly. "What kind of man do you want to be?"

The question caught him off guard. "What do you mean?"

"In your life, in your relationships—what kind of man do you aspire to be? Not what kind of man you think others expect, but who you want to be, authentically."

Kareem thought about his father—stoic, reliable, sometimes distant but always there when it mattered. He thought about Devon—charismatic, unapologetic about taking what he wanted. He thought about himself at twenty-two, earnest and hopeful, believing he could build a life with someone who truly saw him.

"I want to be honest," he said finally. "I want to be brave enough to ask for what I need. I want to be the kind of man who doesn't hide parts of himself to keep the peace." He took a deep breath. "But I also want to be loyal. To keep my promises. To not give up when things get hard."

Dr. Harper smiled slightly. "Those don't have to be contradictory, you know. Honesty and loyalty can coexist. In fact, true loyalty requires honesty."

The timer on Dr. Harper's desk chimed softly.

"Think about that question this week," she said, closing her notebook. "What kind of man do you want to be? And ask yourself if your current choices align with that vision."

As he stood to leave, she added, "And Kareem? Being seen is not too much to ask for."

The memory hit him as he navigated afternoon traffic—not one he'd thought about in years. Their first Valentine's Day, three months after they'd started dating. He'd assumed Fallon would dismiss the holiday as commercial and trite, but she'd surprised him.

He'd arrived at her apartment to find the door slightly ajar, a trail of small origami hearts leading from the threshold to her tiny dining area. The table had been set with candles and takeout from his favorite Ethiopian restaurant. And Fallon—always so composed, so carefully put together—had been wearing heart-shaped earrings, a small concession to whimsy that had touched him more than grand gestures could have.

"I know it's cheesy," she'd said, looking suddenly uncertain. "But I wanted to do something..."

"Perfect," he'd finished for her, pulling her close. "You did something perfect."

Later that night, curled together on her too-small couch, she'd told him about learning origami from a Japanese exchange student in high school—one of those small, unexpected details that made a person real, knowable.

Where had that Fallon gone? The one who could be silly and vulnerable, who shared pieces of herself without calculating the risk?

The car behind him honked, jolting him back to the present. The light had turned green. He accelerated, pushing the memory away.

Twenty minutes later, Fallon Campbell sat at an upscale eatery across town, sipping sparkling water and checking her watch.

"Sorry I'm late," Jessica Collins said, sliding gracefully into the seat across from Fallon like she owned the place—which, with her energy, she just might have. Her natural hair framed her face in a sleek, chin-length bob, and she wore a crisp ivory blouse, vintage shades, and jeans that probably cost more than Fallon's entire brunch tab. Jessica was the closest thing Fallon had to a best friend—fifteen years strong, from undergrad parties to law firm late nights to her new life as corporate counsel for a rising tech giant.

Fallon closed the brief she'd been reviewing and glanced at her watch. "You're only eight minutes behind your personal best. I was starting to worry you'd gone soft."

Jessica gave her a slow, knowing smile. "And you brought a legal brief to brunch. Again. Who hurt you?"

Fallon arched a brow. "Normal people don't make partner by thirty-five."

"Normal people don't want to," Jessica replied, reaching for the menu

"Touché." Jessica smirked, then flagged down the waiter. "Mimosa, please. Heavy on the 'mosa.'" She turned back to Fallon, her expression softening just a little. "So, how are things?"

"Fine. The Henderson merger is—"

"Not work," Jessica cut in smoothly. "You. How are you? How's Kareem? Life outside that corner office?"

Something flickered across Fallon's face—a momentary tightening around the eyes that most people would have missed. But Jessica had known her too long.

"What was that?" Jessica asked, gently but directly. "What happened?"

"Nothing happened," Fallon said, a little too quickly, lifting her glass for another sip. "Everything's fine."

"Mm-hmm." Jessica studied her friend. "You know, for a woman who destroys witnesses on the stand, you're a terrible liar in real life."

Fallon sighed. "I may have... forgotten our anniversary yesterday."

"Girl.." Jessica sat up straighter. "No, you didn't.

"I did." Fallon adjusted her napkin, aligning it precisely with the edge of the table. "It's not a big deal. Kareem made dinner, we ate, life goes on."

"Not a big deal?" Jessica's mimosa arrived, and she took a long sip. "Fallon, it's your anniversary. Seven years, right? That's a big deal."

"It's an arbitrary date on a calendar," Fallon said dismissively. "Kareem knows how busy I am with the Henderson merger. He understands."

"Does he, though?" Jessica leaned forward. "Understanding is one thing. Buttttt......"

Fallon's face tightened almost imperceptibly. "We're not doing this today, Jess."

"Doing what?" Jessica asked, her tone easy, but her eyes sharp. "Asking you to talk about something real for once instead of hiding behind contracts and court dates? Come on now."

"You just don't understand what it takes to make partner. The hours, the sacrifice—"

"Oh, honey... I understand perfectly," Jessica cut in. "I also understand that you use work as a shield to avoid dealing with anything emotional. Always have."

The waiter approached to take their orders, providing a brief reprieve from the conversation. Fallon ordered her usual salad, dressing on the side. Jessica went for the French toast, extra syrup.

When the waiter left, Jessica's expression softened. "Fallon... I'm not coming at you. I'm worried about you. You and Kareem used to have something solid. Real. Now it feels like... like you're scared to let him see you."

Fallon's fingers tensed around her water glass. "That's ridiculous."

"Is it? Because from where I'm sitting, it feels a lot like déjà vu. Like your mom after your dad walked out.""

"Don't," Fallon warned, her voice dropping dangerously low. "This has nothing to do with my parents."

"It has everything to do with them," Jessica countered gently. "You're so afraid of becoming your mother that you've built your whole life around not needing anybody. Not even your husband."

Fallon looked away, her eyes focusing on a point somewhere beyond Jessica's shoulder. When she spoke again, her voice was quieter.

"You didn't see my mother, Jess. After he left. She couldn't get out of bed for weeks. I had to make my own meals, get myself to school, figure out how to pay bills with the money he sent." She shook her head.

"She gave him everything—her heart, her trust, her whole self—and he destroyed her with it."

"And you think that's what Kareem would do? That loving him fully would wreck you like that?"

Fallon's laugh was hollow. "Maybe not intentionally. But that's how it works, isn't it? You open yourself up, become vulnerable, and then... they leave. Or they change. Or they stop caring." She straightened her silverware with precise movements. "I'm just protecting myself."

"What you're doing isn't protection." Jessica reached across the table, covering Fallon's hand with her own. "And you're not just hurting yourself—you're hurting Kareem too."

Fallon pulled her hand away, the rare moment of openness already receding. "Kareem is fine. Our marriage is fine."

"Have you asked him that?" Jessica challenged. "Have you actually talked to your husband?"

Before Fallon could answer, their food arrived. The conversation shifted to safer topics—office gossip, Jessica's new condo, plans for the summer. But Jessica's questions lingered in the air between them, unanswered.

As they were finishing, Fallon's phone rang. She glanced at it, frowned slightly, and declined the call.

"Your dad again?" Jessica asked.

Fallon nodded, her expression unreadable. "Third time this month. I don't know what he wants after all these years, but I'm not interested."

"Maybe he's trying to make amends."

"Too late," Fallon said flatly. "Twenty-two years too late."

Jessica studied her friend. "You know... at some point, you're gonna have to deal with this. Not for him—for you"

"I'm dealing with it just fine," Fallon said, signaling for the check.

"No, Fallon. You manage it. There's a difference." Jessica's voice was gentle but firm. "And at some point, Kareem's going to realize he's paying the price for wounds he didn't cause."

Fallon didn't respond, but for just a moment, something like fear flickered in her eyes.

Back at home, Kareem sat at his desk, reviewing spreadsheets for Monday's meeting. The house was quiet—Fallon had texted that she was meeting Jessica for brunch, then heading to the office. Another Saturday spent apart.

He stared at the rows of numbers without really seeing them, Dr. Harper's question echoing in his mind. What kind of man did he want to be?

His phone chimed with a notification. Probably Devon with some follow-up advice, he thought. Or maybe Fallon with another update about her ETA.

But when he glanced at the screen, his heart nearly stopped.

LinkedIn: Sarah Winters has sent you a message

With suddenly unsteady fingers, he tapped the notification.

Kareem! Just got back in town after three years in Chicago and saw you're still at Barrington Wolfe International. Love to see it. Would love to catch up over coffee sometime. So much to share. Hope life's been good to you

He stared at the message, memories flooding back. Sarah Winters. His college girlfriend. The woman he'd almost proposed to before she'd taken that internship in Paris and they'd decided a long-distance engagement was too much pressure.

Sarah, who'd known him better than almost anyone. Who'd seen him—really seen him—in a way that felt like a distant memory now.

Before he could overthink it, he typed a response:

Sarah, great to hear from you! Coffee sounds perfect. Next week?

He hit send, then sat back, wondering why his heart was beating so fast, and why it felt like he'd just stepped off a cliff.

CHAPTER THREE

REKINDLED

"You sure about this, bro?" Devon asked, setting down the barbell with a metallic clang that echoed through the nearly empty gym. It was 6:30 AM on Wednesday, their standing workout time for the past five years. The early hour meant they practically had the place to themselves—just how Kareem liked it.

Kareem kept a steady rhythm on the treadmill next to Devon's bench, his footsteps tapping in time against the thump of DMX blasting through the gym speakers. "It's just coffee, man. Catching up with an old friend."

Devon grabbed his towel, wiping sweat from his face before fixing Kareem with a knowing look. "Old friend? Man, stop it. Sarah wasn't no 'friend'—you two were out here actin' like y'all was two clicks away from a registry at Macy's before she packed up and went all 'Bonjour' on you."

Kareem adjusted the incline on the treadmill, pushing himself a little harder. "That was a lifetime ago."

"And now she just happens to reach out right when things with Fallon are..." Devon let the sentence dangle meaningfully.

"Coincidence," Kareem said, though he didn't entirely believe it himself.

Devon laughed, shaking his head as he walked over to the bench press. "Man, cut it out with that coincidence stuff. She wants that old thing back—and she ain't slick about it, either."

Kareem slowed the treadmill, wrapping up his run. "You're a fool. But... you might be onto something."

Devon grunted as he pushed the barbell upward. "I'm just saying, people have a way of showing up when you need them most." He racked the weights and sat up, locking eyes with Kareem. "Tell me this—when's the last time someone was genuinely happy to see you walk in the room? I mean lit up like Christmas when you walked in? When's the last time

Fallon smiled at you like that when you came home? Be real, man."

The question hit Kareem harder than Devon probably intended. He grabbed his towel, wiping his face to hide whatever expression might have crossed it.

"It's just coffee," he repeated, more to himself than to Devon.

Devon clapped him on the shoulder as they headed toward the locker room. "Keep telling yourself that." His voice softened a bit. "Listen, I'm not saying go out here and do something stupid, alright? I'm just sayin g... don't be so scared to let something good happen. You hear me? You deserve to be seen, man."

Deserve to be seen. The exact words Dr. Harper had used in their last session.

The coffee shop downtown was bustling with mid-morning activity when Kareem arrived. He'd chosen Leopold's deliberately—it was fifteen blocks from his office and twenty from Fallon's firm, minimizing the chance of running into anyone they knew professionally. A small voice in his head questioned why that mattered if this was just an innocent catch-up between old friends.

He'd arrived fifteen minutes early, a habit Fallon always teased him about ("The world won't end if you're not ridiculously punctual, Kareem"). He claimed a small table by the window, ordered a black coffee, and tried to look casual while checking his watch every few minutes.

At precisely 10:30, the door opened, sending the small bell above it into a cheerful jingle. Sarah stood in the entrance for a moment, scanning the room before her eyes found his. The smile that spread across her face was genuine, unguarded—the kind of smile that reached her eyes and created small creases at their corners.

Something shifted in Kareem's chest at the sight of her. She wore a cream-colored blouse tucked into high-waisted pants, gold hoop earrings catching the light as she moved toward him. Her hair was different—shorter, more sophisticated than the long braids she'd worn in college—but her walk was the same. Confident, unhurried, like she was exactly where she was meant to be.

"Kareem Campbell," she said, her voice warm with genuine pleasure.

He stood, uncertain for a moment about the appropriate greeting. A handshake seemed too formal, but was a hug too familiar? Sarah solved the dilemma by stepping forward and embracing him briefly, the scent of her citrus perfume bringing back memories he hadn't accessed in years.

"Sarah," he said, returning the hug before they both stepped back. "It's good to see you."

"You too." She settled into the chair across from him, studying his face. "Still Mr. Early, huh? Let me guess—you've been sitting here all polished and punctual for, what... ten minutes?"

"Fifteen," he admitted with a small smile.

Sarah laughed, the sound bright and unrestrained. "Some things never change." She glanced at his coffee. "Still taking it black too?"

"Some things never change."

"Well, I've elevated," she said with a playful smile. "These days, it takes at least three kinds of plant milk and a dash of cinnamon magic before I even call it coffee."

When the server appeared, Sarah ordered exactly that—an oat milk latte with a splash of almond milk, cinnamon on top. The complexity of the order made Kareem smile. This was the Sarah he remembered—specific about what she wanted, unapologetic about asking for it.

"So," she said once the server left, folding her hands on the table. "Catch me up. Last I heard, you were putting a ring on Fallon—the law student from that alumni mixer, right?"

"That's right," Kareem nodded. "Seven years ago now."

"God, has it been that long?" Sarah shook her head in disbelief. "Time is wild. And she's a lawyer now?"

"Senior associate at Ellis Grant. On track for partner."

"Impressive," Sarah said, nodding appreciatively. "And you? Still at Barrington Wolfe International?"

"Senior analyst now," Kareem confirmed. "What can I say? Stability looks good on me."

"I always knew you'd do well," Sarah said. "You had that perfect balance of smart and steady. Not flashy, just consistently excellent."

The compliment felt good—specific, personal, not the generic praise he usually received. "What about you? Creative director at Apex now, right? That's a major role."

"It is," Sarah acknowledged with a hint of pride. "Chicago was kind to me, career-wise. Three years of building their Midwest client base from the ground up. Now they've brought me back to help revamp the creative department here."

“That’s amazing, Sarah. But then again, you’ve always had a way of leaving me speechless.”

Her coffee arrived, and she took a moment to appreciate it before continuing. "The career? That’s been the smooth part, honestly. But the personal life..." She let out a soft, knowing laugh, equal parts charm and vulnerability. "Whew—let’s just say life’s handed me some lessons I didn’t know I signed up for."

"I heard you got divorced," Kareem said carefully. "I'm sorry."

Sarah nodded, a shadow crossing her face before she composed herself. "Calvin and I tried. For three years, we really tried. But sometimes trying isn't enough, you know?" She took a sip of her coffee. "We wanted different things, ultimately. He wanted Chicago suburbs, golden retriever, 2.5 kids. I wanted to keep climbing, maybe live abroad again."

"That's tough," Kareem meant it.

"It was the right call." Her voice was calm but sure. "No sense dragging something out when your heart knows better." She smiled, her energy shifting. "But that's enough about my past—let's talk about you. Kids? White picket fence? You living that 'dream home in the suburbs' life you always used to talk about?"

"We have the house," Kareem said with a small smile. "In Woodcliff. No kids yet—Fallon's career has been the priority."

Sarah studied him over the rim of her coffee cup. "And how's that going? The marriage, I mean."

Kareem hesitated, unsure how to answer. The practiced response—"Great, couldn't be better"—hovered on his lips. But something about Sarah's direct gaze made platitudes impossible.

"It's..." he began, then regrouped. "Fallon's brilliant. Driven. She's going to make partner before forty, which is almost unheard of."

Sarah didn't respond immediately, just continued watching him with those perceptive eyes. "You've always done that, Kareem." she said finally, her voice gentle. "Tried to make things sound better than they were."

The observation landed like a stone in still water, sending ripples through Kareem's carefully maintained composure. "What do you mean?"

"Remember senior year, when your dad was sick?" Sarah tilted her head, tone gentle but teasing. "You had everybody thinking he was on the upswing—even when you knew better. You always were good at keeping things polished on the outside." She reached across the table, her fingers brushing his wrist, lingering just a second longer than necessary. "You deflect when you're hurting, Kareem. Start bragging on everybody else, like we won't notice you're the one going through. But I see you. I always have."

Kareem looked down at her hand on his wrist, the simple human contact creating a warmth that spread up his arm. When was the last time Fallon had touched him like this—casually, affectionately, without agenda or obligation?

"I'm not—" he started to protest, then stopped himself. "It's complicated," he admitted finally.

"Life usually is," Sarah said, withdrawing her hand but maintaining eye contact. "You don't have to pretend with me, Kareem. Never did."

That was true, he realized. With Sarah, he'd always been able to be himself—uncertain, imperfect, human. No need to be the steady, dependable rock that everyone else relied on. No need to maintain the façade of having everything under control.

"Enough about me," he said, deflecting again despite himself. "Tell me about Apex. What kind of work are you doing there?"

Sarah allowed the subject change, launching into an animated description of her latest campaign for a sustainable fashion brand. Kareem found himself leaning forward, drawn in by her enthusiasm and the way her hands moved expressively as she talked.

"Remember how you used to help me practice my presentations in college?" she asked with a smile.

"Ah yes, the all-nighter for Professor Simpson's final presentation. Your computer crashed the night before it was due." Kareem nodded. "You were running on coffee and determination. A lesser mortal would've folded."

"You're the only reason I passed that class," Sarah laughed. "And oh my God—remember that janky seafood place we found on the beach trip? The one with the—"

"Neon crab sign and questionable health rating," Kareem finished, smiling at the memory. "Ended up being the best meal of the trip."

"And your first apartment," Sarah added, "where your 'chef phase' almost got you evicted. I still remember that burnt lasagna incident like it was yesterday."

"You remember all that?" he asked, surprised and touched.

"Of course I do," Sarah said simply. "Those were important days. You were important to me."

The words hung in the air between them, loaded with unspoken meaning. Kareem glanced at his watch, startled to see they'd been talking for nearly two hours.

"I should get back to the office," he said reluctantly.

"Of course," Sarah nodded, gathering her things. "This was really lovely, Kareem. Honestly... it felt good. Really good"

They walked outside together, pausing awkwardly on the sidewalk. The spring air was warm, carrying the scent of blooming cherry trees from the nearby park.

"I'm glad life has been kind to you, Kareem," Sarah said, meeting his eyes directly. "You deserve happiness." She reached out, her hand resting briefly on his arm.

The simple touch, the casual validation of his worth—it created something dangerous in Kareem's chest. A longing so acute it was almost painful. To be seen. To be known. To matter to someone as more than a provider, a steady presence, a reliable husband who wouldn't rock the boat.

"I'd like to do this again sometime," he heard himself say.

Sarah's smile was warm but careful. "I'd like that too." She took a business card from her purse and handed it to him. "My personal cell is on there. Text me anytime."

He watched her walk away, the card feeling impossibly heavy in his hand.

The rest of the day passed in a blur of meetings and spreadsheets, but Sarah's words kept echoing in Kareem's mind. "You deserve happiness." Such a simple statement, yet it had landed with the force of revelation. Did he deserve happiness? And if so, what was he willing to do to find it?

By six o'clock, he was heading home, mentally planning the dinner he'd promised to make. Fallon had texted earlier that she'd be home by seven—a rare early evening that he'd been looking forward to. Maybe they could actually talk tonight. Really talk, not just exchange information about schedules and bills.

His phone buzzed as he pulled into their driveway. Fallon.

Henderson meeting running late. Don't wait up for dinner. Sorry. Miss you.

The last two words caught him off guard – a small, unexpected glimpse of the woman he'd fallen in love with. And yet, there was still no mention of their plans. No acknowledgment that they'd specifically scheduled this evening to spend time together. Just another cancellation, another night alone in their perfect house, with those two words that felt both genuine and insufficient.

Kareem sat in the car for a long moment, the engine off, staring at the text. The familiar disappointment settled in his chest, but this time it was accompanied by something else. Anger. Not the hot, explosive kind, but a slow-burning ember that had been quietly growing for longer than he cared to admit.

Inside, the house was quiet and immaculate, just as they'd left it that morning. Kareem moved through the rooms, turning on lights against the gathering darkness outside. In the kitchen, he opened the refrigerator, staring at the ingredients he'd bought for their dinner. Salmon. Asparagus. The exceptional wine he'd splurged on.

He closed the refrigerator without taking anything out and opened a cabinet instead, reaching for the bourbon he kept for special occasions. This wasn't a special occasion, but it suddenly felt necessary.

The amber liquid burned pleasantly as he took a sip, carrying it with him to the living room. Through the French doors, he could see clouds gathering, the spring sky darkening with the promise of a storm. The weather had been like this all week—beautiful mornings giving way to turbulent evenings, the atmosphere charged and unstable.

Kareem sank into the couch, pulling out his phone. Sarah's business card lay on the coffee table where he'd placed it earlier. Elegant, minimalist design. Sarah Winters, Creative Director. And beneath that, her personal cell number, written in blue ink in her distinctive handwriting.

He picked up the card, running his thumb over the embossed letters of her name. It would be so easy to text her. To say he'd enjoyed their conversation. To suggest maybe lunch next time. So easy, and so dangerous.

Outside, the first drops of rain began to fall, tapping gently against the glass doors. The wind picked up, bending the branches of the maple tree in their backyard. In the distance, thunder rumbled—still far off, but approaching.

Kareem set down his glass and picked up his phone, opening his contacts. He typed "Sarah Winters" in the name field, then carefully entered her number from the card. His thumb hovered over the "Save" button for a long moment before he pressed it.

Then, before he could talk himself out of it, he opened a new message.

It was great seeing you today. Thank you for...

For what? Being kind? Seeing him? Reminding him what it felt like to be truly connected to another person?

He deleted the text without finishing it. Too much, too soon. Too honest.

The rain was coming down harder now, beating a steady rhythm against the roof. Lightning flashed, briefly illuminating the darkened backyard, followed by a crack of thunder much closer than before. The storm was moving in fast.

Kareem's phone buzzed with a new notification. Not Fallon—Devon.

So??? How'd it go with Sarah? She still fine? She still feeling you? Details, man!

Kareem smiled despite himself, typing back: *Just coffee. Catching up.*

Devon's response was immediate: *Yeah right. "Just coffee" I know that look you had at the gym. Coffee today, dinner next week, and then...*

It's not like that, Kareem replied, though he wasn't entirely sure that was true.

It could be tho, Devon shot back. *If you wanted it to be.*

Did he want it to be? The question hung in Kareem's mind as another flash of lightning lit up the room, followed almost immediately by a thunderclap that rattled the windows. The storm was directly overhead now, mirroring the tumult in his own thoughts.

On the coffee table, his phone lit up. A LinkedIn notification from Sarah.

Really enjoyed seeing you today... way more than I expected. Let me know when you're free again.

Kareem stared at the message, reading it over and over as rain lashed against the windows and thunder shook the house. His finger hovered over the reply button, a response already forming in his mind.

In that moment, suspended between loyalty and longing, between the safety of the familiar and the allure of the unknown, Kareem felt something shift inside him—something fundamental giving way, like the first crack in a dam that had been holding back too much for too long.

Outside, the storm raged on.

Chapter Four

Fault Lines

Fallon stood at the kitchen island, scrolling through emails on her tablet while absently stirring her morning coffee. The house was quiet except for the distant sound of the shower running upstairs. Kareem had already been gone when she woke, his side of the bed cold. A morning run, she assumed, though he hadn't mentioned it the night before.

She frowned, trying to remember the last actual conversation they'd had. Three days ago? Four? They'd been like ships passing in the night lately—her late work hours, his sudden increase in "networking events." Things felt off, but she couldn't quite place it.

She heard Kareem's footsteps on the stairs. He appeared in the kitchen doorway, already dressed for work in a crisp blue shirt and charcoal slacks, his expression neutral as he reached for the coffee pot.

"Morning." She watched him carefully. "You were up early."

"Gym," he replied, not meeting her eyes. "Devon's been on my case about slacking off."

"Ah." She took a sip of her coffee. "I've got the firm's charity gala today, then the Henderson conference call tomorrow at three."

"I'll probably be late tonight," Kareem said, checking his watch. "Meeting a potential client for lunch, then drinks after work."

Fallon nodded, ignoring the prickle of unease at how easily he'd said it. Kareem had never been one for after-work drinks. That had always been her territory.

"Don't wait up," he said, tossing her own familiar line back at her.

The irony wasn't lost on Fallon. She watched as he poured coffee into a travel mug, grabbed his keys, and headed for the door.

"Kareem," she called after him, surprising herself. He paused, looking back at her expectantly. For a moment, she wasn't sure what she wanted to say. "Have a good day," she finished lamely.

An expression flickered across his face—disappointment, maybe?—before he nodded and walked out.

Fallon stared at the empty doorway, wondering why she suddenly felt like she was losing her grip on something important.

Fallon arrived precisely twelve minutes early to the law firm's charity gala, a strategic timing that allowed her to appear dedicated without seeming overeager. The hotel ballroom was still being prepared, staff arranging centerpieces and adjusting lighting while early attendees in evening wear milled about with champagne flutes.

She smoothed an invisible wrinkle from her tailored black dress and surveyed the room with the calculated assessment she brought to everything—identifying senior partners, potential clients, and convenient exits. Her diamond studs caught the light as she turned her head, the only adornment besides her wedding band.

"Already scoping the room, huh?" Jessica materialized beside her, resplendent in a deep burgundy gown that complemented her warm brown skin.

"Not scoping. Preparing," Fallon replied, accepting the glass of champagne Jessica offered. "Unlike some people, I prefer not to leave professional opportunities to chance."

"And there it is—the armor. You're usually good for at least one drink before it goes on." Jessica observed, clinking her glass against Fallon's. "You're breaking records tonight."

Fallon frowned slightly. "What armor?"

"The 'I'm Fallon Campbell completely self-sufficient legal warrior' routine." Jessica's tone was light but her eyes were knowing. "You usually save the full emotional lockdown for after the second drink."

Fallon opened her mouth for a sharp retort, then hesitated, an unfamiliar feeling shifting inside her. "Kareem isn't coming," she said instead, the words emerging before she'd fully formed the thought.

Jessica raised an eyebrow, clearly surprised by the unprompted personal information. "Out with family?"

"No." Fallon took a precise sip of champagne. "He just said he had 'plans' tonight. Didn't elaborate."

"And you didn't ask," Jessica said, not a question but an observation.

"It's not unusual. We both have busy schedules." Fallon's tone was matter-of-fact, but she couldn't quite meet Jessica's eyes. "Besides, these firm events bore him."

“Please. They bore everybody.” Jessica gestured toward a group of associates forcing laughter at a partner's joke. "That's not the point, though. Kareem used to come to everything, boring or not."

Fallon's fingers tightened slightly around the stem of her glass. "He's been... different lately." The admission felt like a small surrender, a crack in her carefully maintained facade.

Instead of pouncing on the revelation, Jessica simply nodded. "How so?"

"Less available. Less..." Fallon searched for the right word, finding refuge in professional language. "...acc ommodating to scheduling adjustments."

"Wait—so he finally stopped bending over backwards to fit into your career schedule?" Jessica asked bluntly.

Fallon's instinct was to deflect with a cutting remark, to redirect the conversation to safer territory. But Jessica's question had struck too close to a worry she'd been trying to ignore.

"He's been meeting with more clients after work. Networking lunches. He's never cared about that aspect of the business before." Fallon's voice remained controlled, but there was a thread almost like uncertainty beneath it.

"And how does that make you feel?" Jessica asked, studying her friend's face.

"Feel?" Fallon gave a short laugh. "It's not about feelings. We're both professionals with demanding careers."

"That's not what I asked."

"What would you like me to say, Jessica? That I'm concerned? Worried? Jealous?" Fallon's tone took on an edge. "That would be irrational and counterproductive."

"It would be honest," Jessica countered gently.

"It would be weak," Fallon snapped, then immediately composed herself, glancing around to ensure no one had overheard. "Besides, I'm sure it's nothing. Just a phase."

Jessica studied her for a long moment. "You know what's wild? You're more comfortable with the possibility of your marriage changing than with expressing that you might actually care."

"Please—that's ridiculous, and you know it." Fallon said, though the denial felt hollow. "And this little soap opera moment? Yeah, we can dial the drama all the way down."

""Mmm-hmm. And there it is." Jessica said with a sad smile. "Right on schedule. The second it gets real, you slap a 'dramatic' label on it and shut down. Classic Fallon."

"I'm not shutting down. I'm being realistic." Fallon caught sight of a senior partner entering the ballroom. "Richard's here. I need to speak with him about the Peterson brief."

She was already stepping away when Jessica caught her arm, the unexpected contact stopping her mid-stride.

"Have you asked him?" Jessica asked quietly. "Have you actually talked to your husband about why he seems different?"

The question hung in the air between them, uncomfortably direct. Fallon felt a flash of irritation at being cornered, at having her carefully constructed narrative challenged.

"Our communication is just fine, thank you very much." Her voice was stiff.

"That's not what I asked."

"Jessica, please. We're grown, not teenagers passing notes asking if someone likes us," Fallon said, defaulting to the biting wit that had always served as her shield. "Now if you'll excuse me, I need to—"

"You're scared," Jessica interrupted, her voice gentle but unflinching. "You're terrified that if you ask, he might actually tell you the truth."

The words sliced clean through Fallon's composure. She blinked, momentarily thrown, her breath catching just slightly—just enough for Jessica to notice. That unsettling mix of anger and fear began to rise in her chest. She masked it, as always, with control.

"This is not the place, Jess. I have a reputation to uphold," Fallon said tightly. "People are watching."

"They always are." Jessica's tone softened. "But at the end of the night, who are you going home to? And for how much longer?"

Without waiting for a response, Jessica squeezed her arm once more and walked away, leaving Fallon standing alone with a half-empty champagne glass and the uncomfortable weight of questions she'd been deliberately avoiding.

She watched as her friend joined a group of associates, effortlessly sliding into their conversation with a warm smile. Then, with practiced composure, Fallon straightened her shoulders and made her way toward Richard Peterson, burying the momentary vulnerability beneath her professional persona.

But Jessica's words lingered, an unwelcome echo she couldn't quite silence.

You're terrified that if you ask, he might actually tell you the truth.

Across town, at a small lounge with exposed brick walls and soft jazz playing in the background, Kareem sat across from Sarah, watching as she gestured animatedly while describing her latest creative campaign.

"...and I kid you not," Sarah said, her eyes wide with playful disbelief, "the client looks me dead in the face and goes, 'I love it... but can we make the logo bigger?'" Sarah rolled her eyes dramatically. "As if that's ever the solution to anything."

Kareem laughed, relaxing into the moment. This was their third "meeting" in two weeks, each justified as professional networking, though the conversation had strayed far from work topics each time.

"Sounds like my boss when I present quarterly projections," he said. "'But what's the bottom line?' As if that's the only thing that matters."

"Exactly!" Sarah leaned forward, her eyes bright with shared understanding. "It's all numbers and metrics with those types. No appreciation for the people behind it all."

The waiter appeared with their entrées, momentarily pausing the conversation. When he left, Sarah's expression turned more thoughtful.

"Can I tell you something?" she asked, her voice lower, more intimate. "Something I haven't really told anyone else?"

"Of course." Kareem set down his fork, struck by the sudden shift in her demeanor.

Sarah took a breath. "You remember when I said my ex and I wanted different things?" She gave a small, almost imperceptible smile, more sad than amused. "That wasn't the full story." Her eyes dropped to the edge of her plate. "The truth is... I wanted kids. He didn't."

Kareem blinked in surprise. "But I thought—"

"I know what I said before," she began softly, her smile faint, touched with something bittersweet. "It's easier to say we wanted different things than to admit the truth." She paused, her gaze dropping slightly. "I wanted a family. And he just kept... moving the finish line. First it was after the promotion, then after we bought the house, then maybe in a few more years."

She exhaled gently, not bitter, just tired. “One morning I woke up and it hit me—he was never going to be ready. And I was running out of time to start over.”

"I'm sorry," Kareem said softly, genuinely moved by her vulnerability. "That couldn't have been easy."

"It wasn't." Sarah looked up, meeting his eyes. "The hardest part wasn’t the divorce—it was facing the truth. Realizing I’d spent years holding on to the version of us I wanted to see... not the one that was actually there."

The words landed with unexpected weight. Wasn't that exactly what he'd been doing with Fallon? Telling himself things would improve, that her emotional distance was temporary, that once she made partner, once the big case was over, once, once, once...

"Anyway," Sarah continued, reaching for her water glass, "that's my deep, dark confession. “Sorry to drop all that on you."

"Don't apologize," Kareem said. "I'm glad you told me."

As she set her glass down, her hand brushed against his on the table. Neither pulled away immediately, the brief contact lingering for one heartbeat, then two. An electric current passed between them—acknowledgment of a boundary being tested, perhaps crossed.

Sarah was the first to pull back, her expression softening as she glanced down for a beat. Her tone stayed light, but something flickered beneath the surface—words she didn't say out loud. "Anyway... enough about my not-so-happily-ever-after." She looked back up, easing the tension with a half-smile. "Tell me about that client presentation you're working on."

The moment passed, but its weight lingered—unspoken yet present, just beneath the surface of their conversation for the rest of the meal.

Two hours later, Kareem sat nursing a drink and replaying every moment of the evening when Devon slid into the booth across from him at their usual after-work bar.

"Lemme find out you out here havin' another dinner with the ex." Devon's voice carried a knowing undertone. "Sound like you out here sampling the specials."

Kareem shot him a warning look, glancing around to make sure no one they knew was within earshot. "It's not like that."

"Yeah, alright... sure it ain't," Devon replied with a smirk. "That's why you're sitting' here looking' like somebody caught you sneaking out the back door." He waved the bartender over. “Two beers, please, and make sure they are cold this time."

Kareem opened his mouth to deny it, then closed it again. What was the point? Devon had always been able to read him, even back in college.

"Nothing's happened," Kareem said instead. "We're just talking."

"Mmhmm." Devon leaned back as the beers arrived. "See, that's how it starts.'We just talking. Then it's ‘just coffee.’ Next thing you know it's ‘just lunch,’ ‘just drinks,’ ‘just one lil kiss to see if the spark still sparkin’... and BOOM—somebody butt-naked regretting life choices!"

Kareem took a long sip of his beer, the cool bitterness a welcome distraction from the turmoil in his mind. "I shouldn't be spending time with her at all. It feels... disloyal."

"Disloyal?" Devon scoffed. “Man, please! Some marriages just dont work emotionally." He leaned in. "You think I would have made it this long with Vanessa if I ain’t had a side piece keeping’ me sane? Shoot, I’d be somewhere curled up in a ball, humming’ spirituals!"

Kareem stared at his friend, jarred by the casual confession. He'd suspected Devon's fidelity issues ran deep but hearing him admit it so openly was jarring.

"You're cheating on Vanessa?" Kareem asked, his voice low.

Devon shrugged, unrepentant. "Look, man—I don’t cheat. I supplement. You hear me? Like vitamins. You missing something at home; you gotta get your nutrients somewhere!" He took a pull from his beer. "Vanessa ain’t looked at me like a snack since Blockbuster was still open. We've got the house, the friends, and the joint accounts. But the connection? That flame's been out a long time ago."

"So why stay married?"

"Lemme tell you somethin'—divorce? That mess is expensive, messy, and a straight-up headache. Ain't neither one of us tryna burn down the whole house." Devon leaned in, lowering his voice just enough. "So I get what I need on the side, and Vanessa? She gets to keep her picture-perfect life with a husband who stays in his lane and don't ask for nothing. That ain't betrayal, man—that's survival! I'm out here trying to live!"

Kareem felt a knot forming in his stomach. Was that where he and Fallon were headed—a hollow marriage maintained for appearances while they sought real connection elsewhere?

"That's not me," he said firmly, though something inside him wavered.

Devon studied him for a moment. "Maybe not. But let me ask you something. Is it better to sneak around trying to get what you need or sit there playing' loyal to somebody who don't even see you no more?"

Kareem had no answer for that.

Later that evening, Kareem arrived home to find Fallon already there, a rare occurrence these days. She sat at the kitchen island, still in her black dress from the gala, scrolling through her phone.

"You're home," he said, surprise evident in his voice.

She looked up. "The gala ended early. Alert the media—apparently miracles do happen."

An awkward silence fell between them, the kind that never used to exist. Kareem set his keys on the counter, Devon's words still echoing in his mind.

Some marriages just don't work emotionally.

A resolve formed inside him—a decision to try once more, to reach for the connection they'd once had before giving up entirely.

"I was thinking," he said, forcing casualness into his tone, "maybe we could take a weekend trip soon. Get away from the city, just the two of us."

"A trip? When?" Fallon's brow furrowed slightly.

"I don't know. Weekend after next, maybe? We could drive up to that lake house we liked last year."

She was already shaking her head before he finished speaking. "Mm-mm, nope. The Henderson briefs are due that Monday, and I need the weekend to finalize everything."

"The weekend after, then."

"That's the partners' retreat."

"The following weekend?"

"Kareem," Fallon sighed, her impatience showing. "I don't have a crystal ball, and I'm not about to pencil in a weekend fantasy five weeks out. Why the sudden need for a getaway?"

The dismissal in her tone—the way she treated his suggestion as an inconvenience rather than an opportunity—ignited an anger in Kareem. The slow-burning ember of resentment that had been smoldering for months suddenly flared.

"Because we barely see each other anymore," he said, his voice tight. "Because I can't remember the last time we had a real conversation. Because I'm trying to save our marriage before it's too late."

Fallon stared at him, clearly taken aback by his outburst. "Oh, come on. Dramatic much? We're both booked and busy—it's called being grown. This is a phase, not a crisis."

"A phase?" Kareem laughed, the sound hollow. "Fallon, we've been living like roommates for years. This isn't a phase—it's who we've become."

"That's not fair," she said, Jessica's warning echoing in her mind. "I'm working toward something important—"

"And I'm not?" he challenged. "My work matters too. My feelings matter. Our relationship should matter."

"Of course it matters," Fallon said, though her tone was flat, like she was reciting lines she'd practiced too many times.

"Does it?" Kareem stepped closer, suddenly needing to know. "Do you even want me in your life anymore?"

The question hung in the air between them, raw and dangerous. Fallon's expression shifted from surprise to something harder, more defensive.

"Don't be dramatic." Her voice was cool and controlled. "Of course I want you in my life. I just can't drop everything for a spontaneous weekend getaway because you're feeling neglected."

The words cut deeper than outright anger would have. *Dramatic. Neglected.* As if his feelings were childish, inconvenient, unworthy of serious consideration.

In that moment, Kareem understood exactly what Devon had meant—the quiet ache of being in a relationship where your emotional needs are treated like an afterthought, as if they barely mattered at all.

"I need some air," he said quietly, turning away before she could see the hurt in his eyes.

"Kareem—" Fallon began, an unfamiliar note of uncertainty in her voice, but he was already heading for the door, keys in hand.

He drove aimlessly at first, with no destination in mind beyond *away*. The city lights blurred past his windows as his mind replayed Fallon's dismissive words. *Don't be dramatic.* As if wanting emotional connection from his wife was somehow unreasonable.

When he finally paid attention to where he was, Kareem realized with a start that he was in Sarah's neighborhood. Had he unconsciously driven there, or was it genuine coincidence? He couldn't be sure anymore.

He found himself slowing down as he approached her apartment building—a renovated warehouse with large windows and a small courtyard out front. Light shone from what he guessed was her unit on the third floor.

Kareem pulled over and parked, leaving the engine running. His hands stayed on the wheel, but his mind was already inside—already imagining the scent of her perfume, the way she might open the door with a soft smile and a glass of wine in hand, music playing low in the background. No expectations. No accusations. Just... welcome.

What was he doing here?

What was he hoping for?

He didn't have an answer—only a feeling. That ache in his chest, that hunger to be touched without obligation, to be *wanted*, not out of duty but desire. He hadn't felt that in a long time. He sat there for twenty minutes, his phone burning a hole in his pocket. It would be so easy to text her, to say he was outside, to ask if he could come up. So easy, and so irreversible. So dangerous. So final. He sat with it—let the silence stretch, let the engine idle, let the possibilities haunt him. He could almost feel her hands on his shoulders, her eyes meeting his without judgment. But when he looked at his reflection in the rearview mirror, all he saw was a man on the edge of a decision he couldn't undo.

With a sigh that felt like surrender and restraint all at once, Kareem put the car in drive and headed home.

The house was dark when he returned, except for a small lamp in the entryway that Fallon always left on when one of them was out late. He moved quietly up the stairs, not wanting to wake her if she was already asleep.

She was, or at least pretending to be. Her back was to his side of the bed, her breathing measured and even. Kareem changed silently in the dark and slipped beneath the covers, careful to maintain the invisible boundary that had come to define their sleeping arrangements.

He lay awake, staring at the ceiling, wondering how they'd come to this—two people sharing a bed but existing in completely separate worlds.

His phone vibrated softly on the nightstand. He reached for it automatically, the screen illuminating the darkness.

Sarah: *You've been on my mind... Just wanted to say—you deserve better. And you know it.*

Kareem stared at the message, its simple directness piercing through the fog of confusion and hurt that had enveloped him all evening. *You deserve better.* The same sentiment Devon had expressed, the same thing Dr. Harper had implied in their sessions.

Did he? Or was he simply failing to appreciate what he had—a successful wife, a comfortable life, stability and security? Was he being ungrateful? Unreasonable? Dramatic?

He glanced over at Fallon's sleeping form, so close physically yet seemingly unreachable. Then back at Sarah's message, a lifeline of emotional connection being extended across the darkness.

Kareem didn't reply to the text. But he didn't delete it either.

Chapter Five

Crossed Boundaries

"How often have you been texting Sarah now?" Dr. Harper asked, her voice neutral as she made a note in her leather-bound journal.

Kareem shifted in his seat. After months of therapy, he'd become familiar with Dr. Harper's techniques—the way she could ask a simple question that unraveled something complex, the strategic pauses that invited deeper reflection. Still, this one made him uncomfortable.

"I don't know," he said, then caught himself. Therapy only worked with honesty. "A few times a day. Sometimes more." Kareem said.

Dr. Harper nodded, her expression carefully unreadable. "And what do you talk about?"

Kareem offered a small, easy shrug. “Oh, you know ... the usual—work, film, literature.” He paused, then leaned back slightly, his tone dropping. “And occasi onally... the complicated nuances of matrimony.”

"I see." Dr. Harper set her pen down. "And what do you tell Sarah about your marriage that you haven't shared with Fallon?"

The question landed like a stone dropping into still water. Kareem hadn't thought about it that way—that he was sharing intimacies with Sarah that he was withholding from his wife.

"I guess... how I feel. How lonely it's been. How tired I am of always being the one who tries." The admission felt both freeing and shameful. "Sarah sees me—really sees me—in a way Fallon... just doesn’t anymore."

"Or in a way Fallon hasn't been given the opportunity to," Dr. Harper suggested gently.

Kareem frowned. "What do you mean?"

"I'm wondering if you've given Fallon the same chance to hear these feelings that you've given Sarah." She leaned forward slightly. "In our previous sessions, we talked about your tendency to avoid conflict with Fallon, to hint rather than state your needs directly."

"Because every time I try, Fallon puts up a wall like I'm cross-examining her in court and shuts down," Kareem said, defensive heat rising in his voice.

"Perhaps. But there's a difference between being shut down after a genuine attempt at vulnerable communication and avoiding the conversation entirely because you anticipate being shut down." Dr. Harper's tone remained gentle but firm. "I notice that in our recent sessions, we're talking more about Sarah and less about strategies for reconnecting with Fallon."

Kareem looked away, unable to meet her gaze. She was right, of course. When had Sarah become the focus of his thoughts rather than repairing his marriage? The shift had been so gradual he'd hardly noticed it happening.

"I didn't plan this," he said quietly.

"Few people do," Dr. Harper replied. "But we always have choices about how we respond to our circumstances, Kareem. And right now, you're at a crucial decision point."

"What do you mean?"

"You're at a crossroads," Dr. Harper said calmly. "One path leads toward recommitting to your marriage—which would require difficult conversations, vulnerability, and possibly rejection. The other path leads toward deepening your connection with Sarah—which offers validation, excitement, and novelty, but also potential consequences for your integrity and self-image. The real question is: which risk are you willing to take?"

Kareem didn't have an answer. All he knew was that when his phone lit up with a message from Sarah, something in him came alive again—a feeling he'd nearly forgotten was possible.

Sarah: *Had a dream about you last night. Nothing scandalous...just talking by the ocean. Woke up missing your voice.*

Kareem smiled at his phone, warmth spreading through his chest as he sat at his desk. The quarterly reports he'd been reviewing suddenly seemed far less important.

Kareem: *Talking by the ocean sounds peaceful... but now you've got me wondering what you're not saying. Should I be nervous about the director's cut of that dream?*

He sent it before he could second-guess himself, then immediately wondered if he'd crossed a line. This had been happening more frequently in their exchanges—subtle flirtations, hints at attraction, the kind of messages that would make him uncomfortable if Fallon saw them.

Sarah's response came quickly: *That's for me to know and you to wonder about. At least until dinner tonight. Still on for 7?*

Kareem: *Yeah.*

He set his phone down and tried to refocus on work, but his mind kept drifting to Sarah—her laugh, the way she leaned forward when he spoke as if every word mattered, how she remembered details about his life that even Fallon had forgotten.

His desk phone rang, startling him from his thoughts. It was Devon.

"What's good, man?" Devon's voice carried through the line. "You free for lunch? Need to talk to you about something."

"Sure. Usual spot at 12:30?"

"Aight then. And Kareem? Come by yourself.." Devon chuckled at his own dramatic delivery before hanging up.

"Look here, man," Devon said around a mouthful of burger. "You need a whole new email address. I'm talking witness protection level. Don't use no birthdays, no pet names, no favorite songs—none of that! Fallon'll crack that in five minutes while making coffee and arguing a case!"

They were seated at their usual corner table at Mitchell's, a diner far enough from both their offices to minimize the chance of running into colleagues. Kareem had barely touched his club sandwich, his appetite diminished by the conversation.

"I'm not having an affair," Kareem insisted, though the protest sounded hollow even to his own ears.

Devon arched an eyebrow. "Oh, so them texts I saw on your phone when you went to the bathroom—those was just friendly hellos, huh? 'Had a dream about you last night'? Man, get outta here with that!"

Kareem felt heat rise to his face. "You looked at my phone?"

"Man, you acting' like I had to be Inspector Gadget to see that phone light up. Her name popped up big as day, come on now!" Devon leaned forward. "Look, I ain't judging, I'm advising. If you're going to slide down that slippery slope—and let's not kid ourselves, you're halfway down already—at least be smart about it. Don't be out here messy and stupid."

"Smart about what? We're just talking."

"For now," Devon said with certainty. ""But trust me—it's goin' somewhere. And when it do? You better move like the CIA. Separate email, cash only—no paper trail! And don't be taking her to places you and Fallon done been. That's how folks get caught up and end up on Judge Mathis!"

Kareem shook his head, a knot forming in his stomach. "You make it sound so calculated."

"Because it is," Devon replied. "Look, I've been playing this game a long time. The worst mistake you can make is thinking you're special—that somehow you'll be the one who doesn't get caught because your feelings are so real." He took a sip of his soda. "Feelings is exactly what gets people busted. Every. Single. Time."

"I shouldn't be doing this," Kareem said quietly, more to himself than to Devon.

Devon's expression softened slightly. "Hey, Fallon clocked outta your marriage a long time ago. You're just now waking up to it. You ain't out here doing anything' wrong, bruh—you just tryna breathe and survive."

"But the secrecy, the lies—"

"Are necessary. " Devon finished for him. "Man, let me tell you something. The world don't care about context. You could be sitting' there starving' for affection, talking' to walls, feeling' like a ghost in your own house—and the minute you say, 'I found somebody who actually listens to me,' BOOM! You the bad guy!"

The worst part was that Devon's words offered exactly the absolution Kareem craved—a framework that cast his actions not as betrayal but as understandable, even justified. It made the guilt easier to manage, the boundaries easier to cross.

"I don't know," Kareem said, but his protest had weakened considerably.

Devon seemed to sense his wavering. "Just be careful, that's all I'm saying. And if you ever need an alibi for a weekend away..." He winked.

Kareem didn't respond, but he didn't reject the offer either. Another boundary blurred, another step down a path he'd once sworn he'd never take.

Fallon Campbell was not a woman who missed details. As a senior associate specializing in corporate law, she had built her career by noticing the small mistakes that other people ignored. It was this attention to detail that had made her an asset to the firm, positioned her on the fast track to partnership, and now, ironically, alerted her to the shifting dynamics in her marriage.

The changes had happened slowly: Kareem's sudden interest in his appearance, the new cologne, the unexplained absences, and most tellingly, the way he guarded his phone.At first, Fallon thought he was just going through a phase—perhaps prompted by their recent arguments. But as the patterns solidified, a more concerning possibility had taken root.

She sat in their home office late on a Thursday afternoon, having left work early with a migraine that wasn't entirely fabricated. The house was quiet, Kareem not expected home for hours. His laptop sat on the desk, closed but not locked—he'd been rushed that morning, forgetting both his lunch and, apparently, his usual digital precautions.

Fallon stared at the computer. She'd never been the type to snoop, had always valued privacy even within marriage. But the fear gnawing at her overrode principle.

She opened his laptop quickly, wasting no time. His password was still saved—another oversight. His email opened automatically, revealing nothing unusual in the main account. But then she noticed the tab for his LinkedIn account.

Her heart hammered as she clicked on it. The inbox loaded, displaying dozens of exchanges with one predominant contact: Sarah Winters.

I haven't stopped thinking about lunch yesterday. The way you looked at me across that table...It's been a long time since I've been looked at like that.

You make me laugh in a way I didn't realize I missed. Thank you!

Sometimes I wonder what would have happened if we'd never lost touch after college...

The messages grew increasingly intimate as Fallon scrolled backward, documenting a connection that had clearly moved beyond professional networking. None crossed the line into explicit territory, but the emotional intimacy was unmistakable—and in many ways, more threatening than a purely physical affair would have been.

What cut deepest were Kareem's responses:

Being with you... it's different. Feels like I've been holding my breath for a long time and didn't realize it until now."

You understand me in ways I'd stopped expecting to be understood.

Not gonna lie... your messages? They've become the part of my day I actually look forward to.

A notification chimed on Kareem's laptop. When she checked it, Sarah's name appeared on the screen:

Can't wait to see you tonight. Reservation confirmed for 7. Wear that brown shirt I like—the one that matches your eyes.

Cold clarity washed over Fallon. This wasn't speculative. This wasn't paranoia. This was happening.

She put everything back exactly the way it was, making sure no trace of her search remained. Then, with the careful focus she had used many times before in her legal work, she began to plan her response.

"Let's say, purely hypothetically..." Fallon kept her voice carefully casual as she stirred her coffee, "at what point does emotional infidelity constitute grounds for divorce?"

Across the table, Marcus Bennett raised an eyebrow. As one of the firm's top divorce attorneys, he'd heard variations of this question countless times, though rarely from fellow lawyers.

"Well, that all depends—on the state, the situation, and let's be honest... how sharp the other side's lawyer is," he replied, studying her with newfound interest. "Why? Client issue?"

"Friend of mine," Fallon said smoothly. "She recently discovered her husband has been... emotionally involved with another woman. Texts, secret meetings, the classic pattern. She's weighing her options."

Marcus nodded, not entirely convinced by the "friend" pretext but professional enough not to challenge it. "Alright... let's say this is about a friend. Then here's what your friend needs to do—start keeping a record. Everything. Text messages, emails, credit card receipts, dinners, gifts, anything that shows a pattern. And write it all down which includes dates, times, and what was said. Suspicion's one thing. But if she wants to be taken seriously, she's going to need facts. Solid facts. That's how you build a case."

"And what about confrontation? Should she confront him directly or wait?"

"Well... that depends." Marcus leaned back. "If she's looking to salvage the marriage, then yes, confrontation with the possibility of counseling. If she's decided it's over, then strategic preparation before any confrontation is wiser." He leaned forward slightly. "So the real question is... what does your friend want?"

The question caught Fallon off guard. What did she want? The automatic answer—to win, to protect herself, to ensure she wasn't the vulnerable one when everything imploded—felt hollow in a way she hadn't expected.

"I don't think she knows yet," Fallon admitted.

Marcus reached into his jacket pocket and retrieved a business card, sliding it across the table. "When she decides, have her call me directly. I'll make sure she's protected, whatever path she chooses."

Fallon took the card, its embossed lettering catching the light. "Thank you. I'll pass this along."

As she tucked the card into her purse, a heavy feeling pressed against her chest. It wasn't the anger she expected. It was something deeper. A quiet kind of heartbreak. She felt it for everything she had lost, for the future that would never happen, and for the painful truth that her first move was to protect herself with a lawyer... not to fight for the love she once believed in.

The restaurant Sarah had chosen was deliberately intimate—a small Italian place with candlelit tables and a renowned wine selection. It was across town from where Kareem and Fallon typically dined, minimizing the risk of running into mutual acquaintances. Another boundary crossed in the name of "discretion."

Sarah was already seated when he arrived.She wore her hair down, and it fell around her face in a way that made her cheekbones stand out. Her eyes lit up when she saw him, a genuine smile spreading across her face.

"You wore the brown shirt," she said as he took his seat across from her.

Kareem felt a rush of pleasure at her noticing. "You said you liked it."

"I do." Her gaze held his a moment longer than necessary. "It brings out your eyes."

The evening flowed easily. They shared appetizers, their fingers occasionally brushing as they reached for the same piece of bread. They talked about books, films, memories from college, and plans for the future—all while carefully avoiding direct mentions of Fallon or the reality of Kareem's marriage.

It was a dance of leaving things unsaid, creating a bubble where only the two of them existed. By the time they ordered dessert to share—a tiramisu with two forks—it was pretty clear their connection was becoming more than just friendship.

"You know," Sarah said, her voice lower after their second bottle of wine, "lately... I've been thinking a lot about the things we wish we could undo."

"What kind of things?" Kareem asked, leaning forward.

"The what-ifs..." she said, her voice low, almost a whisper. Her eyes met his. "Like... what if I hadn't gone to Paris after graduation? What if we'd actually stayed... us?"

The question hung between them, loaded with implications. Kareem felt his heart rate accelerate.

"I've thought about that too," he admitted, the wine making him bolder than he might otherwise have been. "More than I probably should... especially lately."

Sarah's hand moved across the table to cover his. “Is it so wrong,” she said softly, “that I’m actually... grateful you think about it too?”

"No," Kareem said, turning his hand to intertwine their fingers. "It's not terrible at all."

The rest of dinner passed in a heightened state of awareness—each glance, each touch, each shared laugh carrying a new voltage. When the check came, they both reached for it, laughing at the awkwardness.

"This one's on me," Sarah insisted. "You can get the next one."

The next one. The promise of continuation, of furthering whatever this was becoming. Kareem didn't object.

Outside, the spring night was unexpectedly cool, a light rain beginning to fall. Sarah shivered slightly in her sleeveless dress. Without thinking, Kareem slipped off his jacket and draped it over her shoulders.

"Always the gentleman," she said softly, looking up at him with an expression that made his breath catch.

"Old habits," he replied, his hands lingering on her shoulders a moment longer than necessary.

"I'm parked just down the block," she said. "You mind walking me to my car?"

They walked together through the light rain, close enough to feel each other's presence but never quite touching. The air between them buzzed with unspoken tension. When they reached her car, Sarah turned to him slowly, droplets clinging to her lashes like tiny stars.

"I had a wonderful time tonight," she said.

"So did I."

She made no move to remove his jacket or get into her car. Instead, she stepped closer, her eyes on his. "Kareem..."

The way she said his name—soft, questioning, inviting—broke something loose inside him. He closed the distance between them, one hand moving to her face, thumb brushing her cheek. She didn't pull back. Instead, she leaned in, eyes locked to his, her lips parting just enough to invite the inevitable. Their breath tangled, heavy with everything unspoken. The air between them charged like a storm about to break. Kareem felt himself pulled forward, powerless, caught in a current he no longer wanted to resist.

His phone rang in his pocket—Fallon's ringtone. That familiar sound sliced through the moment like a knife, sharp and unforgiving. He froze, his hand still on Sarah's face, their lips still achingly close.

The phone kept ringing. Sarah didn't move, but her expression changed—just slightly. There was a flicker of understanding in her eyes, maybe even disappointment, but not surprise.

"You should answer that," she said softly.

Kareem withdrew his hand and took a step back, reaching into his pocket. Fallon's name and photo lit up the screen. He let it go to voicemail, unable to imagine speaking to his wife in this moment, with Sarah's perfume still clouding his senses.

"I'm sorry," he said, though he wasn't entirely sure what he was apologizing for—the interruption, or the fact that they'd come so close to crossing a line that couldn't be uncrossed.

Sarah smiled, a mixture of warmth and resignation. "Don't be. This is... complicated. I understand that."

The rain began to fall harder, as if the weather itself was intervening to end the moment. Sarah slipped off his jacket and handed it back to him.

"You should go," she said. "Text me when you get home?"

Kareem nodded, not trusting himself to speak. He watched as she got into her car, offering a small wave before driving away. Only then did he check his voicemail.

"Hey, it's me," Fallon's voice came through, unusually subdued. "Just wondering what time you'll be home. Call me back if you get this before eleven."

The guilt hit him as he walked to his own car, a heavy weight in his chest. But alongside it, undeniable and unsettling, was a current of excitement—the thrill of connection, of being wanted, of standing at the edge of something forbidden but compelling.

These conflicting emotions warred within him during the drive home, wipers beating a steady rhythm against the strengthening rain. What kind of man was he becoming? What would happen the next time he saw Sarah, without Fallon's timely call to interrupt? Would he have the strength to pull back again—or did he even want to?

The house was dim when Kareem arrived home. As he hung his wet jacket by the door, he noticed Fallon sitting in an armchair, a glass of red wine in one hand. She hadn't turned at the sound of his entrance, her gaze fixed on the darkness beyond the window where rain lashed against the glass.

"You're still up," he said, trying to keep his voice casual.

"Yes." The single word carried no inflection, offering no clues to her thoughts.

Kareem moved into the room, hyperaware of the lingering scent of Sarah's perfume on his clothes, the wine on his breath, the guilt surely visible in his eyes. "My apologies." He kept his voice casual. "My phone was on silent during dinner."

"Business dinner?" Fallon asked, still not looking at him.

The question was a lifeline—an opportunity to maintain the facade, to retreat into familiar deception. "Yes," he said, the falsehood slipping out with disturbing ease. "Potential client. Looks promising."

Fallon took a slow sip of her wine, the light from the lamp casting a glow on her face. She didn't say anything, and her expression gave nothing away. But the way she sat—still, almost too still—made it clear. She was holding herself together, barely.

"How was your day?" Kareem asked, desperate to shift the focus.

"Predictable." She finally turned to look at him, her eyes moving over his face with an intensity that made him wonder if she could somehow see Sarah's almost-kiss imprinted on his lips. "The same meetings, the same performances. Nothing new.

There was something in her tone—a bitter edge that could have been about the gala, or could have been about something else entirely. Kareem couldn't tell, and the uncertainty left him feeling unbalanced.

"I'm gonna call it a night. Early meeting tomorrow."

Fallon nodded, returning her gaze to the window. "I'll be up shortly."

As Kareem climbed the stairs, relief and anxiety battled within him. The conversation had been brief, superficial—nothing to suggest Fallon suspected anything. Yet something had felt off, a subtle wrongness he couldn't quite identify.

In the bedroom, he quickly changed and went through his nighttime routine, wanting to be asleep—or at least pretending to be—before Fallon came up. Only when he was lying in bed, the room dark around him, did he allow himself to text Sarah.

Home safe. Thank you for dinner. And everything else.

Her reply came almost immediately: *Sweet dreams, Kareem. Think of me.*

He deleted both messages as soon as they'd been sent and received—another new habit in his growing repertoire of secrets.

Downstairs, Fallon remained in the darkened living room, listening to the sound of Kareem moving around upstairs. She took another sip of wine, feeling the warmth spread through her chest without reaching the cold knot that had formed there.

She'd smelled another woman's perfume on his jacket when he'd hung it up. Slowly and carefully, she reached into her pocket and pulled out the business card Marcus had given her. She turned it over between her fingers, watching how it reflected the light from the lamp.

Preparation, not confrontation. Strategy, not vulnerability. These were the approaches that had served her throughout her life—the methods that ensured she would never be blindsided, never be left exposed and devastated as her mother had been.

She slid the card back into her pocket and finished the last of her wine. The house was quiet—too quiet. Only the soft tap of rain against the windows filled the silence. But underneath it all, she could feel it—like a crack spreading through glass. Her marriage wasn't just struggling. It was breaking, slowly and painfully, and there was nothing she could do to stop it.

CHAPTER SIX

PRECIPICE

The law firm of Ellis Grant occupied the top three floors of a gleaming downtown tower, its reception area designed to intimidate with floor-to-ceiling windows and artwork that cost more than most people's homes. Tonight the main conference room had been transformed for the annual Ethics Dinner—white tablecloths, crystal glassware, and floral arrangements created an atmosphere of sophisticated luxury.

Kareem adjusted his tie as he followed Fallon through the crowd of attorneys, judges, and their spouses. These firm events had always made him uncomfortable—the forced smiles, the strategic conversations, the constant game of who's impressing who. But tonight felt suffocating—the close call with Sarah still clinging to him, and the widening gulf between him and Fallon turning every conversation into an act he was too tired to keep performing.

"Richard wants us at table one," Fallon said, her hand barely touching his elbow. "We're sitting with the managing partner, two federal judges, and the ethics committee chair. Major visibility. So sit up straight and smile."

Kareem nodded, understanding what was unsaid. This was a career opportunity for Fallon, a chance to strengthen relationships with people who could influence her path to partnership. His role was simple: look successful, sound intelligent, and above all, make Fallon look good.

"Fallon Campbell!" Richard Peterson's booming voice cut through the crowd as they approached the table. "And the long-suffering Mr. Campbell."

"Good evening, Richard," Fallon replied with a practiced smile. "You remember my husband, Kareem."

"Of course, of course," Richard shook Kareem's hand firmly. "The numbers man at Barrington Wolfe. Still keeping the financial ship afloat?"

"Doing my best," Kareem said, forcing a smile.

"Come, sit. Judge Garcia was just telling us about his famous test for ethical dilemmas."

They took their places at the table, Fallon immediately engaging the judge in conversation while Kareem exchanged pleasantries with the other spouses. He knew this routine all too well—standing on the sidelines, making small talk while the "important people" had the real conversations.

The dinner progressed predictably through salads and entrées, the discussion moving from casual chatter to more substantial topics as wine flowed. By the time dessert arrived, the conversation had turned to professional ethics—specifically, situations where personal integrity might conflict with client interests.

"The problem with ethics these days," Martin Bennett, the managing partner, said with authority, "is that too many professionals confuse legal with ethical. Just because you can do something doesn't mean you should."

"Precisely," Judge Garcia nodded. "I see it in my courtroom every day. Attorneys technically within bounds but clearly violating the spirit of ethical practice."

"That's an oversimplification," Fallon interjected, her tone politely challenging. "Judges get to sit up high on their moral pedestals, but the rest of us? We're out here juggling egos, ethics, and a dozen different agendas before lunch."

"Are you suggesting ethics are relative, Ms. Campbell?" Judge Garcia raised an eyebrow.

"I'm suggesting they're contextual," Fallon replied smoothly. "What appears unethical from the bench might be responsible advocacy from the bar."

The conversation heated up as partners and judges traded increasingly layered perspectives. Kareem leaned in, his mind turning over ideas about the intersection of personal ethics and professional duty. It wasn't just theory—it hit close to home. As they spoke, he couldn't help but think about Sarah, the temptation he'd nearly given into, and the slow-burning frustration simmering in his marriage.

When there was a natural pause, he spoke up. "Perhaps the real challenge is maintaining internal consistency—ensuring your actions align with your own core values, regardless of external pressures."

A brief silence followed his comment, several heads turning toward him with mild surprise, as if they'd forgotten he was there.

"Interesting perspective," Judge Garcia said thoughtfully. "Though perhaps somewhat... idealistic."

"I'd say naïve," Fallon said with a light laugh that sent ice through Kareem's veins. "My husband tends to see these issues through the simplistic lens of personal finance rather than the complex realities of legal practice."

The dismissal was direct and cutting. Kareem felt heat rush to his face as several people at the table shifted uncomfortably.

"I wasn't speaking about finance," he said quietly. "I was talking about personal integrity."

"Oh bless your little analyst heart." Fallon patted his hand in a gesture that managed to be simultaneously affectionate and condescending. "You have to admit, Kareem. Your run-ins with ethical dilemmas are what we'd call... entry-level. In your world, it's spreadsheets and policy memos. Not exactly the moral minefield we're navigating up here, right, Richard?"

Richard, clearly sensing tension, attempted to smooth things over. "Well, I'm sure financial analysis presents its own ethical challenges—"

"Oh, certainly," Fallon continued, her smile not reaching her eyes. "Challenges like whether to splurge on the deluxe office pens or stick with the budget pack." She turned to the table with a conspiratorial smile. "Kareem once spent an entire weekend weighing the moral implications of a coffee maker. I'm talking full-on internal debate—filters, features, the whole saga. Ethics, brought to you by Consumer Reports."

A ripple of laughter moved around the table. Even those who seemed uncomfortable with her approach felt obligated to respond to her joke. Kareem sat frozen, the public humiliation washing over him in waves.

"I'd argue that ethical consistency is precisely what distinguishes true professionals," Judge Garcia said, mercifully shifting the focus away from Kareem. "Whether in law or finance."

The conversation continued, but Kareem could barely focus. His wife's words kept playing in his head, each time hitting harder. He stayed calm only by forcing himself to, nodding and smiling when needed, even though his mind was stuck on what she had just said.

This wasn't anything new—Fallon had been brushing off his opinions for years. But being embarrassed like this in front of her colleagues, turned into a joke for everyone to laugh at, made everything wrong in their relationship suddenly clear.

When dinner ended and guests began to mingle, Kareem excused himself to the restroom. Alone in the marble-lined space, he gripped the edge of the sink and stared at his reflection. The face looking back seemed different—older, sadder, but clearer. Whatever illusions he'd been maintaining about his marriage had shattered on that pristine white tablecloth.

"Rough moment out there," a voice said from behind him. Richard Peterson was washing his hands at the adjacent sink. "Fallon can be... intense when she's in professional mode."

"Oh, *that's* what we're calling it now?" Kareem replied, unable to keep the edge from his voice.

Richard dried his hands carefully. "For what it's worth, I thought your point was spot-on. Judge Garcia did too. Mentioned it to me after you left." He paused. "Fallon's brilliant, but she sometimes mistakes aggression for strength."

Kareem nodded, not trusting himself to speak.

"Politics," Richard said, as if that explained everything. He clapped Kareem on the shoulder. "Don't take it personally."

But it was personal. That was the whole point. Fallon had taken something personal—their private relationship, his trust in her—and weaponized it for professional advantage. As Kareem walked back into the reception, weaving through small groups of people talking, he kept a friendly smile on his face—even though his mind was suddenly thinking more clearly than ever.

When Fallon finally approached him to leave, she seemed oblivious to his inner state.

"Ready?" she asked, checking her watch. "I think we've put in enough time."

Kareem simply nodded, not trusting himself to speak without saying something they couldn't take back.

The ride home was quiet, the darkness outside matching his internal state. Rain started to fall, sliding across the windshield and making the city lights look blurry and strange. Fallon scrolled through her emails on her phone, acting like she didn't notice the heavy tension coming from his side of the car.

Navigating the wet streets, Kareem mentally cataloged years of similar dismissals, the countless times his feelings had been deemed unimportant, his perspectives invaluable. He thought about Sarah's words—*You deserve better*—and for the first time, he truly believed them. He deserved to be respected, not tolerated. To be seen, not overlooked. To be valued, not taken for granted.

And in that moment, everything became clear—Kareem knew he couldn't keep pretending anymore.

Fallon went straight to the home office when they got back, saying she had a brief to look over before morning. Kareem headed to the bedroom, but the whole house felt different now—like a quiet prison made of fake smiles, things left unsaid, and the feeling that he was living a life far smaller than the one he wanted.

He was sitting on the edge of the bed, staring at nothing, when his phone vibrated with a text from Sarah:

I've been thinking about the other night... a lot. Can you come by? Only to talk—I promise.

He stared at the message, the simple invitation heavy with implication. They both knew "talk" wasn't all that would happen if he went to her apartment tonight. It was a precipice, a point of no return.

Another text arrived before he could respond:

I miss you, Kareem. I miss us.

His finger hovered over the reply field. It would be so easy to say yes, to seek comfort in someone who actually wanted his presence, who valued his thoughts, who saw him as more than an accessory to her ambitions.

With sudden decision, he stood up and grabbed his keys. He wouldn't reply—he would just go. Actions over words. Decision over deliberation.

As he headed for the stairs, Fallon emerged from the office, surprising him.

"Going somewhere?" Her tone was casual but her eyes sharp.

"Out," he said simply. "I need some air."

She studied him for a moment. "It's almost midnight."

“Trust me, I’m quite aware of the time.”

His tone must have registered, because her expression shifted slightly, a flicker of uncertainty crossing her features. "Kareem—"

"I'll be back later," he said, already moving past her toward the stairs. "Or maybe I won't. I haven't decided yet."

He left before she could respond, the door closing with a clear sense that the conversation was over.

In his car, rain hammering on the roof, Kareem pulled out his phone and called Devon. Despite the late hour, his friend answered on the second ring.

"My man! This is either really good news or really bad news," Devon said, music playing faintly in the background. "Don't tell me you locked up, 'cause I ain't got no bail money and I ain't tryna visit nobody through no glass."

"I'm not in jail," Kareem replied, his voice tight. "But I'm about to do something I can't take back."

The music in the background dimmed, suggesting Devon had moved to a quieter location. "Sarah?"

"Yeah. She invited me over."

"And you callin' me for *what*, exactly?"

"I don't know." Kareem gripped the steering wheel with his free hand, knuckles white. "Maybe I need someone to talk me into it. Or out of it."

There was a pause on the other end of the line. "You know what I've been telling you, man. Fallon clocked out a long time ago. She *been* gone, brother. You deserve something for yourself."

"That's what Sarah says too. That I deserve better."

"Smart woman."

Kareem closed his eyes briefly. "So you think I should go?"

Devon's response wasn't immediate this time. When he spoke again, his voice had lost some of its usual bravado. "Let me tell you somethin', man... once you cross that line? That's it. Ain't no round-trip ticket, no refund, no store credit. You in it. Sometimes..." He paused, a weariness creeping into his tone. "Shoot, sometimes I be laying in bed staring at the ceiling like, 'Maybe—just maybe—being honest back then, might've been better than dragging' all these secrets around like old luggage."

Kareem opened his eyes, surprised by the admission. "What do you mean?"

"Look here, Kareem—this game? Man, it gets old. All that lying, sneaking' around, and playing James Bond every time your phone buzz? That stuff will eat you up inside!" Devon shook his head. "Now don't get it twisted—I ain't sayin' don't go. I'm saying' you better be *real* sure this what you want. 'Cause it ain't just one night of fun—it's a whole lifetime of stress, drama, and trying' to remember what lie you told last Tuesday!"

The unexpected vulnerability from his usually cavalier friend gave Kareem pause. "Are you unhappy, Devon?"

"Happy, unhappy... those are big words, man." Devon's voice had regained some of its usual lightness, but a deeper authenticity lingered underneath. "I'm just saying that sometimes that easy choice you make today? Turns into a heavy suitcase you gotta carry for the rest of your life".

After they hung up, Kareem sat in his parked car for several minutes, Devon's words echoing alongside Dr. Harper's question: *What kind of man do you want to be?*

He eased the car into drive and set off, navigating the streets with purpose as he headed toward Sarah's apartment.

Standing outside Sarah's door, hand raised to knock, Kareem felt as if he were watching himself from a distance—a man on the edge of a decision that would alter the course of not just his marriage, but his understanding of himself.

The hallway was quiet, the only sound was the low hum of the building's air conditioning. From a nearby apartment came the scent of something cooking—garlic and rosemary, warm and familiar—a sharp contrast to the weight of the decision he was about to make.

Before he could knock, the door opened. Sarah stood there in jeans and a simple t-shirt, her expression a mixture of surprise and pleasure.

"You came." Her voice was soft. "I wasn't sure you would."

"Neither was I," Kareem admitted.

She stepped back, inviting him in with a gesture. The apartment beyond was warmly lit, a glass of wine already poured on the coffee table, music playing softly in the background. Everything about the scene spoke of intimacy, of expectation.

"Come in," she said. "Please."

Kareem remained where he was, suddenly frozen by the reality of what he was contemplating. Images flashed through his mind in rapid succession: Fallon on their wedding day, eyes bright with promise; Dr. Harper asking what kind of man he wanted to be; Devon's unexpected moment of regret; and finally, his own reflection in the rearview mirror on the drive over, almost unrecognizable to himself.

"I can't," he said, the words emerging with unexpected certainty. "Not like this."

Sarah's expression shifted. "Because you're married?"

"Because this isn't who I want to be." Kareem shook his head. "I've spent months complaining about Fallon's emotional withdrawal, about her dismissal of my feelings, about her failure to fight for our marriage. And here I am, about to betray everything I claimed to value."

"You're not betraying anything," Sarah said gently. "You're just trying to feel something real... something you've been missing for far too long."

"Maybe. But I'd be betraying myself." Kareem met her gaze directly. "I want connection. I want to be seen and valued. But I also want to be the kind of man who addresses problems directly instead of creating new ones. Who doesn't compromise his integrity when it's difficult to maintain."

Sarah leaned against the doorframe, studying him. "So what are you going to do?"

"I don't know yet. But it starts with honesty—with Fallon, with you, with myself." He took a step back. "I'm sorry. You deserve better than this too."

Sarah gave a faint smile, one that didn't quite reach her eyes. "I know," she said softly. "And I'm proud of you for realizing that... even if it hurts."

She stepped back, folding her arms like she was holding herself together. "But if you're choosing the right road... then you can't keep standing at the fork."

A pause. Her voice was steady, but her eyes shimmered. "You should go, Kareem."

"Goodbye, Sarah."

As he made his way back to the elevator, Kareem felt the weight change—a burden lifted, but another took its place.The lie was gone, stripped away, and in its place was the heavier, but clearer, weight of facing the truth head-on.

Fallon hadn't planned to go through Kareem's desk drawer. She'd been looking for a spare charger, moving methodically through the home office when she found the folded papers tucked beneath a stack of financial statements.

Receipts. Therapy receipts, dating back four months. Weekly sessions with Dr. Adrienne Harper, Clinical Psychologist specializing in relationship counseling.

Four months. Sixteen sessions of Kareem pouring out his feelings to a stranger while maintaining a facade of normalcy at home. Sixteen sessions of seeking help while she remained oblivious, wrapped in her own priorities and perceptions.

Fallon sank into the desk chair, receipts spread before her like evidence in a case she hadn't known was being built. The discovery shouldn't have hurt—it was practical, after all, to seek professional help when needed—yet the secrecy itself cut deeply.

Had she been so unapproachable that Kareem couldn't share his struggles? Had she been so dismissive of his feelings that he'd had to find validation elsewhere? The questions were uncomfortable, piercing through her carefully constructed defenses.

Fallon thought about their interaction at the ethics dinner earlier that evening—how quickly she'd dismissed his contribution, how easily she'd diminished him publicly. It hadn't seemed significant at the time, just another moment in their increasingly disconnected lives. But viewed through the lens of these receipts, through the knowledge that he'd been seeking professional help while she'd been charging ahead obliviously, her behavior took on a different cast.

What else had she missed? What other pain had Kareem been carrying while she focused on partnership tracks and case strategies?

For the first time in years, Fallon allowed herself to truly consider her husband's experience—not as an extension of her own life, but as a separate person with needs and feelings she'd systematically overlooked. The realization was uncomfortable, challenging her self-image as a fair and reasonable partner.

The sound of the front door opening snapped her from her thoughts. She quickly gathered the receipts, returning them to their hiding place before moving to the hallway.

Kareem stood in the entryway, rain-soaked and different—a subtle shift in his posture, in the set of his jaw, that suggested a decision had been made.

"You're back," she said, aiming for casual but landing somewhere closer to uncertain.

"Yes." He removed his wet jacket, hanging it carefully. "We need to talk, Fallon."

The words were calm but carried a weight she hadn't heard from him in years. This wasn't the conflict-avoidant Kareem who would swallow his feelings to keep the peace. This was someone new—or perhaps someone familiar, returned after a long absence.

"Okay," she said cautiously. "About what?"

"Not tonight." He shook his head. "I need to think, and you need to sleep. Tomorrow." He met her gaze directly. "Really talk. No deflection, no dismissal, no hiding behind work. Just truth."

Fallon felt a flicker of her usual defenses—the instinct to take control of the conversation, to reframe it on her terms—but the memory of those therapy receipts stopped her. Instead, she simply nodded. "Tomorrow."

Kareem moved past her toward the stairs, then paused. "I'm going to stay at the Marriott tonight. I need some space to think."

"You're leaving?" The words came out sharper than intended, fear disguised as indignation.

"Just for tonight." He turned to face her. "I'm not walking away, Fallon. I'm walking toward clarity. There's a difference."

He continued upstairs, presumably to pack an overnight bag, leaving Fallon standing in the hallway, uncharacteristically speechless.

Twenty minutes later, as the sound of his car faded into the rainy night, Fallon sat looking out the window. The reality of her marriage's precarious state finally, undeniably clear. For years, she had been preparing for betrayal, armoring herself against abandonment, maintaining careful control to avoid vulnerability.

Yet somehow, despite all her preparations and defenses, she found herself exactly where she'd feared—standing alone in an empty house, facing the very real possibility of losing the one person she'd tried so hard not to need.

Chapter Seven

Confrontation

The Marriott hotel room was functionally comfortable but soulless—a king size bed with crisp white linens, a desk with a padded chair, abstract artwork in muted colors. Kareem had slept fitfully, waking multiple times to the disorienting realization that he wasn't home. Each time, the events of the previous evening flooded back—Fallon's public humiliation at the firm dinner, his near-visit to Sarah's apartment, the decision to spend the night away from home.

By morning, exhaustion had settled into his bones, but his mind was surprisingly clear. As he showered and dressed in wrinkled clothing, he mentally rehearsed what he would say to Fallon. Not a script—he'd tried that before, only to have her lawyer's precision dissect his arguments until he forgot his own point—but a framework. The boundaries he would no longer allow to be crossed. The needs he would no longer pretend weren't important.

He checked out at 9:30 AM, deciding against breakfast at the hotel. The drive home was short but significant, each mile bringing him closer to a confrontation he'd been avoiding for years.

What he didn't expect, as he pulled into their driveway at 10:17 AM on a Tuesday, was to see Fallon's car still parked there.

She never missed work. Even when sick with the flu two years ago, she'd conducted conference calls from their bedroom, her voice hoarse but her arguments precise. The fact that she'd stayed home suggested either an emergency or a deliberate choice that made his heart beat faster as he unlocked the front door.

The house was quiet but not empty—a coffee mug on the kitchen counter, a laptop open but sleeping on the dining table, a faint scent of the vanilla bean shampoo Fallon used. Kareem set his overnight bag down and moved through the first floor, finally finding her in the sunroom at the back of the house.

Fallon sat curled in the wicker armchair, wearing yoga pants and an oversized sweater—weekend clothes she'd never normally wear on a weekday. Her hair was pulled back in a simple ponytail, her face bare of makeup. She held a mug of tea between her palms, staring out at the garden where spring flowers were just beginning to bloom. She looked younger somehow, more vulnerable, and for a moment Kareem was reminded of the woman he'd fallen in love with years ago.

She turned as he entered, her expression carefully neutral. "You're back."

"I said I would be." Kareem remained in the doorway, uncertain of his welcome.

"You also said we needed to talk." Fallon set her mug on the side table. "Well, I'm right here. So let's have the conversation."

There was something different about her tone—not the sharp defensiveness he'd expected, but not her usual controlled calm either. He moved into the room, taking the chair opposite hers, the small table between them like neutral territory.

"You're not at work," he said, starting with the obvious.

"I took the day off." She met his gaze directly. "This seemed more important."

The simple statement caught him off guard. When had Fallon last prioritized their relationship over work? He couldn't remember.

"I appreciate that."

A silence stretched between them, neither quite sure how to begin. It was Fallon who finally broke it.

"Oh, I found your therapy receipts."

Kareem stiffened, a flash of indignation rising. "You went through my things?"

"I was looking for a charger," she replied, a defensive edge entering her voice. "And what do I find? Four months of therapy, Kareem. *Sixteen* sessions with Dr. Harper—tucked away in a drawer like a dirty little secret. And not one word. Not one."

"Would you have listened if I had?" Years of accumulated frustration bled into the words.

Fallon started to respond, then stopped herself. "Maybe not." The honesty was unexpected. "But finding out like that... realizing you've been talking to a stranger about our marriage while I had no idea you were that unhappy."

" No idea?" Kareem couldn't contain the bitter laugh that escaped him. "Fallon, I've been trying to tell you for years. You just haven't been listening."

"That's unfair—"

"Unfair?" He leaned forward, the structure of his rehearsed words collapsing as raw emotion began to break through the cracks. "What's unfair was last night."

"Last night," she said quietly, "at the dinner. I was dismissive. Condescending."

"You humiliated me," Kareem corrected, the pain still fresh. "In front of your people—your colleagues, your mentors—the ones you bend over backward to impress. You turned me into a joke. A punchline. Like I was just some fool sitting at your table for decorati on..."

"I didn't mean—"

"Yes, you did." His voice was steady but intense. "And that's the part you don't wanna face, Fallon. You meant it. Maybe not the pain it brought—but the way you brushed me off? That wasn't an accident. That was you setting' me right where you think I belong. Like I'm some afterthought in your grand plan".

Fallon's eyes widened slightly, his directness clearly surprising her. "That's not how I see you."

"Really? Because from where I'm sitting, that's exactly how you've treated me for years. Just some inconvenience getting' in the way of whatever you really got going on. And I'm supposed to sit here and smile, be thankful for the little crumbs of attention you toss my way—between court dates and climbing' that ladder."

"That's not true," she repeated, but with less conviction.

"Nah, see—what's not true... is giving' seven years of your life to somebody who acts like being real with you for five minutes is too much to ask!" Kareem felt something break loose inside him, words he'd held back for so long finally finding release.

Fallon stood up quickly and walked to the window, turning her back to him. When she finally faced him again, her eyes were cold and sharp, like stone.

"Oh, is that why you've been seeing her?" The temperature in the room seemed to drop with her words.

"What?" Kareem felt his stomach tighten.

"Sarah Winters." Fallon's voice was deceptively calm, like the air before a storm. "Your college sweetheart. The one you were oh-so-ready to marry before Paris came calling." She crossed her arms, her posture shifting from vulnerable to prosecutorial in an instant. "How long has that been going on?"

Kareem felt his face flush. "How do you know about Sarah?"

"That's not an answer." Fallon's words were clipped, precise. "How. Long."

"It's not what you think—"

"Really?" A bitter laugh escaped her. "Because what I think is while I've been busting my tail pulling eighty-hour weeks trying to make partner, you're out here rekindling things with your ex."

"We haven't slept together," Kareem said firmly.

"How noble," Fallon snapped, arms crossed and sarcastic. "Am I supposed to clap? Send a thank-you card? Be moved by your sudden display of basic self-control?"

"That's not what I meant—"

"Oh, really? Then what exactly did you mean, Kareem?" She stepped closer, fury and hurt warring in her expression. "Please, enlighten me—how is sneaking off to see your ex-girlfriend behind my back not betrayal? Go ahead, Professor Integrity, explain how that lines up with all your noble speeches about honesty and ethics."

"I was wrong," Kareem admitted, his voice low. "Meeting Sarah... keeping' that from you? That was wrong. Flat-out wrong. There's no excuse for it—and I'm not trying to give you one."

"But?" Fallon prompted, hearing the unspoken qualification.

Kareem met her gaze directly. "But Fallon, this didn't just come out of nowhere," he said, his tone sharp, pained—raw. "I've been drowning in this marriage for years. Trying' to reach for you while you build walls higher and higher. Every time I speak, it's like my words hit a brick. You treating me like I'm the burden. And after a while... a man starts to feel like he doesn't even exist in his own house."

"So this is my fault?" Her voice rose sharply. "The only solution was running to another woman?"

"I'm not saying it's your fault—"

"Because that's exactly what you're saying." Her lawyer training kicked in, words precise and cutting. "Textbook blame-shifting, and honestly? Weak."

"That's not—"

"Let me be clear." Fallon's hand slammed the counter. "You don't get to dump your guilt at my feet. If you were unhappy, you should've said something. Instead you chose secrets."

The accusation hung in the air between them, both truth and distortion in the same breath.

"I get it, and you're right," Kareem said finally. "Meeting Sarah was wrong, regardless of what was happening between us."

The admission seemed to catch Fallon off guard, as if she'd been prepared for a longer fight.

"But let me tell you what you are wrong about," he said, stepping closer, his tone tightening. "I didn't choose her. I was tempted—Lord knows, I was. But when it came down to it, I chose us. I chose to turn around, to walk away. Because I couldn't live with crossing that line."

"You want a cookie for keeping it in your pants?" Fallon scoffed, eyes narrowed.

“No. I don’t want anything.” Kareem exhaled hard, running a hand down his face like he was trying to wipe the night away. His voice dropped, calm but heavy. “I’m just telling you what happened. After the dinner... Sarah invited me to her apartment.” He looked her straight in the eye. “And I went.”

Fallon inhaled sharply, her composure cracking.

“I went to her door,” Kareem said, his voice steady but low. “She opened it. Everything was set up—candles, wine, the whole scene.” He paused, jaw tight. “But I couldn’t do it.” He shook his head, the weight of the moment settling in.

"Why?" The question seemed torn from her, almost against her will.

"Because that's not who I want to be," Kareem said simply. “And even if I did... that wouldn’t fix anything. It wouldn’t heal what’s broken. It’d just make a mess—a whole new set of problems, a whole new list of regrets I’d have to carry.”

Fallon turned away, her shoulders rigid with tension. "So you just expect me to trust you now? After that?"

"I don't know," Kareem answered honestly. "Trust would have to be something I'd have to rebuild with you if we decide to try."

"If," Fallon repeated, the single syllable laden with meaning.

They'd moved to the kitchen without thinking, the conversation following them. Fallon filled the kettle, seeking comfort in routine.

"But you know what the worst part is?" Kareem said, breaking a tense silence. "Sometimes it felt like you were almost daring me to cheat."

Fallon stopped, her hand frozen midway to the cabinet. "Excuse me?"

"The cold shoulder, the shutting down, the way you brushed me off every time I tried to really talk to you." He met her gaze directly. "It's like you were setting the stage for failure—either I sit there starving for connection, or I step outta line and you get to say, 'See? That's why I kept my guard up.'"

Fallon snapped, arms crossed and eyes blazing. "So I'm the villain in your affair story again? You're really standing here trying to say I pushed you into her arms? That is absolutely ridiculous, and you know it."

"Maybe not consciously," Kareem said, his voice steady, eyes locked in. "But on some level—"

“Uh-uh, no.” Fallon cut him off, her eyes flashing. "I didn't lure you into some emotional trap. You made your mess."

"Then what would you call it?" Kareem challenged. "Years of silence between us, years of making me feel like my needs didn't matter—"

"I gave what I had, Kareem. That was my best." Fallon shot back. "Maybe it wasn't good enough for you. Maybe I'm not naturally demonstrative or emotionally available in the way you want. But that doesn't mean I was setting you up to fail."

"Fallon—"

"Listen to me very carefully," she said, her voice deadly calm as she moved closer. "I have never, in seven years of marriage, done anything to deliberately hurt you or push you away. Have I been emotionally guarded? Yes. Have I prioritized work over our relationship sometimes? Yes. Have I struggled to be the kind of partner you seem to need? Clearly." She crossed her arms tightly. "But let's get one thing straight—what I haven't done is play games with your heart or set traps to see if you'd fall in. And I most certainly did not invite you to cheat like it was some test you were supposed to fail.

Kareem opened his mouth to respond, then closed it, recognizing the genuine offense in her expression.

"You don't get to rewrite this narrative," Fallon continued, her voice catching slightly as her composure cracked. Her fingers curled into a fist that she pressed against the counter. "That's not taking responsibility, Kareem. That's finding an excuse."

Her words landed like a slap, cutting through his self-justification. He looked away, uncomfortable with the truth in her assessment.

"You're right," he said finally. "That wasn't fair."

"No, it wasn't," Fallon agreed, but some of the edge had left her voice. She leaned against the counter, suddenly looking tired. A single tear formed at the corner of her eye, which she blinked away with military precision. "I've made my share of mistakes, yes. I'll own that. But what I will not accept—what I will not excuse—is betrayal. That was never supposed to be part of the deal."

" I didn't go looking to betray you, Fallon. That's not what this was." He paused, watching her closely. "And I don't need perfect. I just... I need real. I need you—whatever that looks like."

The kettle clicked off, and Fallon poured water into her mug, her hands trembling slightly despite her efforts to appear composed. She didn't respond immediately, and Kareem had the distinct impression she was carefully considering her next words—weighing them for both impact and self-protection.

"It's not that simple," she said finally, turning to face him, her hands cradling the steaming mug.

"Then explain it to me," Kareem said, leaning against the counter opposite her. "Help me understand."

Fallon's gaze dropped to her tea, then lifted to meet his, something vulnerable flickering in her eyes before her usual composure reasserted itself. ""I'm not sure how to become the woman you keep reaching for in your mind—because I don't know if she's me."

"I'm not asking you to be anybody but who you are," Kareem countered. "But I need all of you—not just the edited version you think I can handle."

"What if those are the only parts I know how to show?" The question emerged softer than her usual tone, a rare admission of limitation.

Kareem studied her, really seeing her—the tension in her shoulders, the careful neutrality of her expression that didn't quite mask the uncertainty beneath. "Why is that, Fallon? What are you so afraid of?"

She moved away from him, set her mug down on the island with a sharp click. "I'm not afraid."

"Yes, you are," Kareem said, following her. "You're afraid to let somebody all the way in. I've watched you lay brick after brick, building a fortress around your heart—and I stood there, trying to wait it out. But I'm not waiting' in silence anymore.. I need to know why. I need to know what you're protecting yourself from..."

"It's not about—"

"Is it about your parents?" Kareem asked, the insight from therapy sessions with Dr. Harper informing the question. "About what happened when they divorced?"

Fallon went very still, her back to him. "That has nothing to do with us."

"I think it has everything to do with us." Kareem moved around the island so he could see her face. "I think you've been running from their example your entire adult life."

“Oh, please. That is absolutely ridiculous, and you know it”

"Is it?" He pressed gently. "Your mother broke down when your father walked out. Since then, you’ve been running. Running’ from becoming her. So scared of needing somebody that you won’t let anybody all the way in. Not even me.”

Fallon's eyes flashed with a mixture of anger and pain. “Don’t you dare psychoanalyze me, Kareem. You have no idea what it was like—none.”

"No, I don't," he acknowledged. "Because you never laid it out for me. I’ve caught bits and pieces over the years—little flashes of the truth—but never the full picture. Never how it sat on your heart. Never how it *really* felt."

"Because feelings don't change anything!" The words burst from her with unusual intensity. "Feelings didn't stop my father from leaving. They didn't get my mother up when depression pinned her to the bed. And they sure didn't put food on the table or keep the lights on when everything around us was falling apart."

The raw emotion in her voice startled both of them. Fallon seemed almost surprised by her own outburst, as if a door had opened that she'd thought securely locked.

"You're right," Kareem said quietly. "Feelings didn't change your situation. But they shaped you, Fallon. They still are. They're shaping *us*. Whether you want to face that or not."

She turned away, her hands gripping the edge of the counter so tightly her knuckles showed white. For a long moment, she said nothing, and Kareem waited, sensing that pushing further would only cause her to retreat.

When she finally spoke, her voice was so quiet he had to step closer to hear.

"I watched her disappear right in front of me," Fallon said, her voice steady but quiet. "My mother—brilliant, elegant, the kind of woman who could command a room with a glance—reduced to... someone I didn't recognize. Couldn't eat. Couldn't sleep. Spent her nights crying, begging a man to come back *after* we found out about the other woman." She paused, her throat tightening, but refused to let the emotion win. A deep breath, a lift of her chin. "I promised myself—*swore*—that I would never let anyone have that kind of power over me. That I would never be so dependent... so vulnerable... that another person's betrayal could break me like that."

"So let me get this straight," Kareem said, voice low, eyes locked on hers. "You've been holding me at arm's length—for seven years—because you're scared of becoming your mother. Scared I'd do to you what he did to her." He shook his head slowly, the weight of it all settling in. "And all this time, you've been punishing' me... for a crime I didn't commit."

Fallon turned to face him, her composure cracking further. "You think I want to be this way?" she said, voice trembling despite her best efforts. "You think I enjoy holding back, second-guessing every feeling, every moment—because deep down I'm terrified that the second I trust it, it'll all fall apart?"

She took a breath, eyes shining. "I didn't ask for this fear. I inherited it."

"But I am not your father, Fallon," Kareem said, his tone softening, the edge in his voice replaced by something deeper. "I have never—not *once*—given you a reason to believe I'd walk away."

Fallon lowered herself into the dining chair, her movements slow, as if the weight of the moment had finally settled into her bones. "This isn't about logic, Kareem," she said quietly, wrapping her arms around herself. "It's not about what you've done or haven't done. It's about fear. Bone-deep, unreasonable fear. That if I let myself lean on you—if I love you completely—I'll lose whatever pieces of me I've fought to hold onto. And then… when you leave—"

"If," Kareem corrected. "If I leave. Which I haven't. I'm still here, Fallon. I'm still trying."

"But for how long?" she asked, the question carrying the weight of her deepest fears. "How long before I become too much? Before you decide I'm more work than I'm worth... that whatever I am—whatever I've been through—is just too complicated to keep loving."

The vulnerability in the question stunned Kareem. Never in their seven years together had Fallon been this open about her insecurities, this transparent about her fears.

"I don't have all the answers," he answered honestly. "But I can promise to try—if you're willing to try too. Really try, not just go through the motions."

Fallon nodded, her usual eloquence deserting her in this moment of raw truth. They sat in silence for several minutes, the weight of their conversation settling around them. The confrontation had revealed more than either had expected—layers of hurt, fear, and misunderstanding that had accumulated over years.

Eventually, they moved into the living room, both worn out in body and mind. They sat at opposite ends of the couch they had picked out together back when things were easier. The space between them felt strange—smaller because they had finally been honest with each other, but bigger because the future still felt so uncertain.

"Where do we go from here?" Fallon asked eventually, the lawyer in her seeking clear direction, a path forward.

"I don't know," Kareem admitted. "I know what I need—real connection, intimacy that means something. I need to feel like I'm not just here, but that I *matter* to you." He paused, eyes searching hers. "But I also know you've been carrying things I can't always see. And maybe you're trying in your own way...but I dont know."

"I don't know either," Fallon said, and the candid uncertainty was itself a kind of progress. "I've spent so long building walls to feel safe... I honestly don't know if I remember how to let someone *in*.

Kareem nodded, appreciating her honesty even as it underscored the difficulty of their situation.

Fallon looked at him directly, her expression more open than he'd seen in years. "Would you be willing to try counseling?" she asked, each word carefully measured. "Together, I mean."

The question hung in the air between them—not a solution, but a possible first step. A recognition that whatever happened next, they couldn't navigate it alone, with the same patterns and behaviors that had brought them to this precipice.

"Yes," Kareem said after a moment's consideration. "I think we owe ourselves that."

Fallon nodded, relief and apprehension mingling in her expression. "I've never done anything like that before," she admitted. "Therapy... counseling... that just wasn't something we did in my family. You prayed, you kept quiet, and you carried on."

"I know," Kareem said. "That's why it means something that you suggested it. That takes courage. And I see it."

They sat together a while longer, the silence between them no longer hostile or evasive, but tentative, cautious. Neither knew if their marriage could be saved, but for perhaps the first time, they were seeing each other clearly—flaws, fears, and possibilities all laid bare.

Later that evening, after Fallon retreated upstairs to take a few work calls—because some habits hold tight, even on a day like this—Kareem found himself alone on the back patio. The sky was a canvas of fading gold and soft rose, the kind of sunset that asked for silence and reflection. He leaned back in the chair, the weight of the day finally catching up with him.

Then his phone buzzed—a text from Devon.

So??? How'd it go, man? She cut you or you still got all your limbs?

Kareem smiled slightly at his friend's attempt at humor, then replied:

We talked. Really talked. Going to try couples counseling.

Devon's response came quickly:

For real?! Now that's a plot twist if I ever seen one. Give it a shot. Just make sure she ain't doin' it for show.

The concern beneath the casual words touched Kareem. Despite Devon's own questionable choices in relationships, he genuinely wanted happiness for his friend.

Thanks, D. I think she's serious. Time will tell.

Kareem set his phone down and turned his face toward the last bit of sunlight. The day had been long—tiring, emotional, and full of hard truths. He didn't know if counseling would work. He wasn't sure if Fallon could really unlearn habits she'd been holding onto for most of her life. And he didn't know if they could truly fix what had already been damaged.

But for the first time in a very long time, they had been honest with each other. No defense, no attitude, no shutting down. Just truth. And while honesty alone doesn't heal a marriage, it's the first step toward something better—whether that's rebuilding or learning to let go.

Tomorrow, the real work would begin. Tonight, they hadn't fixed everything. But they had stopped pretending. And in a marriage that had gone quiet for too long, that was a meaningful start.

Chapter Eight

Excavation

Dr. Adrienne Harper's waiting room was tastefully minimal—soft earth tones, well-cushioned chairs, and lighting that soothed rather than spotlighted. There were no gossip magazines or flashy self-help titles scattered across the table. Instead, a thoughtful collection of literary journals and art books rested neatly in a wooden tray—quietly signaling that this was a space for reflection, not distraction. Substance, not spectacle. A small framed quote on the wall read: "The truth shall set you free—but first it will make you uncomfortable."

Fallon sat stiffly on the edge of the armchair, her lawyer's folder resting on her knees like a shield. She wore her dark gray pantsuit—the one she saved for big court cases—and Kareem noticed she looked more ready for a fight than for fixing anything. Her foot tapped quietly against the wooden floor, the only clue that she was more nervous than she let on.

"You can put the closing argument away, Counselor," Kareem said quietly. "We're not in court."

Fallon's eyes flicked up from the legal pad where she'd been making notes. "What?"

He nodded toward the portfolio. "All these notes. That power suit. Fallon, it's just a conversation."

"Well, excuse me for being prepared," she said, but there was less edge in her voice than there might have been a week ago. "Some of us function better with structure."

Before Kareem could respond, the inner office door opened, and Dr. Adrienne Harper stepped into the waiting room. Her emerald green blouse was the only bright color in the quiet, neutral room. Around her neck, she wore a silver tree of life necklace that shimmered in the light as she walked.

"Kareem," she said with a warm smile, then turned to Fallon with equal warmth. "And you must be Fallon. I'm Dr. Harper. Please, come in."

Fallon rose, extending her hand with the practiced firmness she used for professional introductions. "Dr. Harper. Thank you for seeing us on short notice."

"Of course," Dr. Harper replied, her handshake equally firm but somehow more personal. Her round tortoiseshell glasses sat low on her nose as she studied Fallon for a moment with perceptive eyes. She gestured toward the inner office. "Please, make yourselves comfortable."

The therapy room itself was arranged to facilitate conversation without forcing intimacy. Two comfortable chairs faced each other at an angle, with enough space between them to keep things respectful. A small couch sat along the wall for another seating option, and Dr. Harper's chair was placed to complete a triangle shape. A side table held a water pitcher and some glasses, and bookshelves along one wall showed she was both smart and experienced. African decorations, like a handwoven cloth on the table and a framed piece of kente fabric, gave the room a warm and welcoming feel.

Fallon hesitated for a moment, scanning the room as if locating exits, before choosing one of the chairs.

Kareem took the other, noticing the familiar tension in his wife's shoulders that appeared whenever she entered unfamiliar territory.

Dr. Harper settled into her chair, her posture both relaxed and attentive. "Before we begin, I want to thank both of you for taking this step. Coming to couples therapy takes courage, and it's important that you know that simply being here is already significant."

Fallon shifted slightly, her portfolio still clutched like a shield. "Well, we want to be... proactive."

The corporate buzzword made Kareem suppress a smile. Even here, Fallon couldn't help framing their crisis in terms she might use at the firm.

"That's a good place to start," Dr. Harper nodded, her glasses sliding slightly down her nose. "Marriage, you know, is a lot like tending a garden. You can't just show up when the weeds have taken over—it needs care, intention, and presence every single day." She gently pushed her glasses back up with a graceful touch. "Now, since this is our first time sitting down together—though Kareem and I have had some powerful conversations one-on-one—I'd love to hear from both of you. What brought you here today?"

The question hung in the air, neither rushing to answer. Kareem had been here before, had navigated these waters in his individual sessions, but this felt different—more consequential, with Fallon beside him.

"We've been having some... communication issues," Fallon finally offered, her lawyer's gift for understatement on full display.

Dr. Harper stayed quiet on purpose, letting the silence stretch. She didn't try to fill the space with words, giving the moment a chance to sink in. The quiet itself became part of the therapy, slowly pushing past Fallon's walls.

Finally, Kareem spoke. "What she means is that we've been living like strangers under the same roof for years, and last week it all came to a head."

Fallon's posture stiffened further, but she didn't contradict him.

"Can you tell me more about what 'came to a head' means?" Dr. Harper asked, her tone neutral but engaged.

Kareem glanced at Fallon, wondering how much she was willing to share, how honest this first session would be. To his surprise, Fallon spoke first.

"Kareem spent the night at a hotel after I—let's just say I conducted myself poorly at a professional event," Fallon said, her tone composed and deliberate. "The following day, we finally had an honest conversation—our first in years, if we're being truthful. And no, it wasn't pleasant."

"No, it wasn't," Kareem agreed. "But it was real. Maybe the most real we've been with each other since we got married."

Dr. Harper leaned in just a little, taking off her glasses and looking at each of them with warmth and intention. "Let me tell you something—what you allow in your relationship, you give permission to continue," she said, her voice soft but clear, full of truth. "It sounds like the two of you have been allowing patterns that, quite frankly, have been pulling you apart instead of bringing you closer." She let the moment breathe, then added with genuine curiosity, "So what came out of that conversation that made you think... maybe it's time to get some help?"

Again, Fallon surprised him.

“We’ve both been caught in a pattern that’s been quietly chipping away at us,” she said, her voice calm but honest. “And as capable as we both like to think we are... it’s become clear we can’t fix it by ourselves.”

“That,” Dr. Harper said with a warm, affirming nod as she slid her glasses back on, “is a powerful place to begin. So many couples walk through this door with one person playing the victim and the other cast as the villain. But what you’ve just acknowledged? That you both play a role in the story—that matters. Because marriage isn’t about finding someone to complete you. It’s about two whole, grown people making the choice—every day—to show up, to grow, and to walk this journey together.”

Kareem felt a small measure of relief at the therapist's validation. Maybe this could work after all.

"Since you mentioned patterns," Dr. Harper continued, “I’d love to hear what patterns you’ve each noticed in your relationship. Kareem, you’ve had a bit more experience with therapy, so why don’t you lead us off?”

Kareem took a deep breath, aware of Fallon tensing beside him. "I think... the pattern is that Fallon keeps her distance emotionally—maybe as a way to protect herself. And I haven't pushed back on it. I've gone along with it for the sake of peace, telling myself that was love. But the truth is, I was avoiding conflict, and in doing that, I lost pieces of myself. Over time, that turned into resentment".

"Resentment that almost led you to another woman," Fallon added, unable to keep the edge from her voice. "Let's not skip that part."

Dr. Harper's expression remained neutral, though her attention sharpened. "What I'm hearing," she said gently, "is that trust has been broken somewhere along the way.

Kareem nodded slowly, his voice steady but heavy. "Yeah... I reconnected with somebody from my past. An ex. Nothing happened—physically. But it was going there. And I knew better. I stepped back before it crossed that line, but still... it was wrong. And I own that. All of it."

"I appreciate your honesty," Dr. Harper said warmly, her voice calm and grounded. "That gives us something real to work with." She turned gently toward Fallon, her tone inviting. "Now tell me, from where you stand—what patterns have you been seeing?"

Fallon uncrossed her legs and then recrossed them, her fingers tightening slightly on her portfolio. "I don't do emotional displays. That's not withholding—that's just who I am," she said, carefully choosing her words. "He thinks I'm withholding, but it's not deliberate. It's just... how I operate. How I've always operated."

"Has it always been that way for you?" Dr. Harper asked. "Even before your relationship with Kareem?"

"Yes," Fallon said quickly, then paused. "Well—mostly. It got stronger after college, I think. But even as a child, I wasn't the type to wear my heart on my sleeve. That's just never been me."

"Last week, you mentioned your parents," Kareem said quietly. "About how their divorce affected you."

Fallon shot him a look that might have silenced him a week ago, but he held her gaze steadily.

Dr. Harper leaned in gently, her voice warm and thoughtful. "Would you be open to exploring that?" she asked. "Because so often, the way we love—and the way we struggle to love—can be traced back to the family we came from. That's where so many of our patterns begin."

Fallon was quiet for a long moment, her fingers unconsciously tracing the edge of her portfolio. "When I was twelve..." She stopped, then started again. "My parents' marriage ended badly. My father left for another woman, and my mother... didn't handle it well."

"Can you help me understand what 'didn't handle it well' looked like?" Dr. Harper asked gently.

Fallon's gaze fixed on a point somewhere beyond Dr. Harper's shoulder. "She collapsed. Completely. Depression, couldn't get out of bed some days. Crying all the time. Begging him to come back even after we knew about the affair." Her jaw tightened. "I was twelve, and suddenly I was the one making sure bills got paid, food was in the house, that she didn't..." She stopped abruptly.

"That she didn't harm herself?" Dr. Harper supplied quietly.

Fallon gave a slight nod, her composure threatening to crack for just a moment before she reinforced it. "She never actually attempted anything, but there were... comments. Enough that I was afraid to leave her alone some days."

Kareem felt a surge of compassion despite his own hurt. In their seven years of marriage, Fallon had never shared this level of detail about that period of her life.

Dr. Harper leaned in gently, her voice warm but clear. "That's a heavy, heavy weight for a child to carry. And I want you to really sit with that for a moment. How do you think carrying that shaped the way you show up in your relationships today?"

Fallon let out a sharp, brittle laugh. "Isn't it clear? I made a decision a long time ago—I would never let myself be that vulnerable. I wasn't going to build my life around anyone else's presence or approval." She paused, her voice tightening. "I watched my mother lose herself—completely—in my father. And when he left..." Fallon shook her head, her composure slipping just slightly. "I swore I'd never let that be me."

"So what you did," Dr. Harper said gently, her voice full of knowing, "was turn emotional independence into a shield. It became your way of surviving—of making sure no one could ever hurt you that deeply again."

"Exactly." Fallon met the therapist's eyes directly, perhaps recognizing a kindred spirit in Dr. Harper's calm self-possession.

"And yet," Dr. Harper continued, her voice gentle but probing, "you made the choice to marry Kareem. You made the choice to create a lifelong partnership—one that, by its very nature, invites connection, shared responsibility, and yes... interdependence."

The comment lingered in the space between them, exposing a contradiction Fallon clearly wrestled with. Dr. Harper remained quiet, giving Fallon room to feel the weight of the tension and reflect on the uncomfortable truth it revealed.

"I loved him," she said finally, her voice softer. "And I thought... I thought I could have both. The stability of marriage without opening myself up to the kind of hurt that broke my mother."

"But it doesn't work like that," Kareem said, his voice low, tight with hurt. "You want the title, the picture-perfect life—but not the weight that comes with it. See, you've been trying to play it safe, keeping one foot in and one foot out. But real love? Real connection? That takes risk. That takes investment.

Fallon's eyes flashed. "That's not fair. I have invested in this marriage—financially, practically, in every tangible way. Just because I don't process emotions the way you do—"

"It's not about processing differently," Kareem cut in. "It's about sharing at all. You don't let me in, Fallon. You never have. Not really."

Dr. Harper removed her glasses, a gesture that immediately captured both their attention. "“Real connection,” she began, “comes from a place of wholeness—from overflow—not from emptiness or desperation.” She looked at Fallon, then at Kareem, her gaze steady and full of grace.

"Now let’s take a breath and step back. Kareem, you’ve shared that you often feel like Fallon holds back emotionally. And Fallon, you’ve opened up about how being emotionally independent was something you learned—something that helped you survive after watching your mother’s pain. You see, both of those things can be true. They don’t cancel each other out. They actually help us understand the full picture."

She replaced her glasses, her gaze softening. "You know, it’s interesting how the very things that draw us to someone can later become the things that challenge us the most. Kareem, maybe it was Fallon's independence and strength that first caught your heart. And Fallon, maybe it was Kareem's emotional openness that made you feel safe. But now? Those same beautiful traits are pushing you apart. It's not uncommon—it's just part of the deeper work relationships ask of us."

Both nodded reluctantly, the insight landing visibly.

"Now, Kareem," Dr. Harper continued, balancing her attention equally between them, "you mentioned that you may have played a part in enabling this pattern. Let's go a little deeper—can you share what that looked like in your marriage? What role did you play in allowing it to continue?"

Kareem shifted in his chair, uncomfortable with the spotlight turning to his contribution. "I... I guess I've always been that guy who keeps the peace. Always have. That's how I was raised—be the calm in the chaos, the one who fixes things, holds it all together. When I met Fallon, her strength, her drive—I respected that. I loved that. But somewhere along the way, that strength turned into distance. And I saw it happening. I felt it. And I stayed quiet. I should've said something sooner.

"Because?" Dr. Harper prompted.

Kareem locked eyes with Fallon, his voice steady. "See, by staying quiet, I was telling you it was okay to keep shutting me out. Like that distance between us was something I could live with—but I couldn't." He leaned in slightly, the weight of his words landing heavy. "I kept thinking... if I just loved you harder, waited long enough, maybe—maybe—you'd finally feel safe enough to stop hiding behind that wall."

Did he really think I ever felt safe enough to let go? The thought flashed through Fallon's mind, surprising her with its clarity—and its sadness.

"But instead," Kareem continued, "I showed you there were no consequences. I kept giving out grace like it was endless—like you could just take and never pay it back. And you did. Over and over again."

"And this pattern reminds me of something you mentioned in our individual sessions," Dr. Harper noted. "About your friend Devon's influence on your thinking about marriage."

Fallon's attention sharpened. "Devon? You mean Mr. Smooth-Talker who can't keep his eyes—or hands—to himself whenever Vanessa turns her back? That Devon?"

Kareem sighed. "Yeah... that Devon. We've had some real talks—deep ones. About marriage, expectations, all of it. He's been dealing with his own mess with Vanessa."

"By 'dealing with,' you mean cheating on," Fallon said flatly.

"Fallon," Dr. Harper said softly, her tone calm but firm, "let's take a moment and give Kareem the space to share why his friendship with Devon matters here. This is part of his truth, and it deserves to be heard."

Kareem rubbed the back of his neck, uncomfortable but committed to honesty. "Devon's been... I guess you could say he's been my counterpoint. He's always saying things like 'This is just how marriage is after a while' or 'You can't expect to get everything from one person.' And for a while, I think I was starting to believe him."

"In what way?" Dr. Harper asked.

"That maybe emotional disconnection was just... part of the deal. Like wanting' more made me ungrateful or something. Like I was askin' for too much." He met Fallon's eyes. "And when I started thinking about connection somewhere else... he made it seem like that wasn't betrayal. Not if I was starving at home."

Fallon's expression hardened. "So he encouraged your relationship with Sarah."

"I'm not going to say all that" Kareem admitted. I'm not going to blame him for my choices—they were mine—but his perspective had an influence. Made it easier to justify crossing lines I shouldn't have crossed."

Dr. Harper leaned forward slightly. ""Kareem, I want you to really think about something. In our one-on-one sessions, you've talked a lot about your values—how much integrity matters to you, how deeply you believe in doing what's right."

She paused, letting it settle. "Now ask yourself this: Has Devon's way of handling his marriage—seeking connection outside instead of facing what's broken on the inside—brought him peace? Has it made him truly happy?"

The question hit harder than Kareem expected. He pictured Devon's forced laughter, the tightness that always seemed to fill the room when he and Vanessa were around each other, the way Devon's late-night texts had become more frequent—full of complaints, frustration, and silent regret about his marriage.

"No," he said finally. "I don't think he is happy. He puts on a good show, but... no."

"I've seen them together," Fallon said unexpectedly. "Devon and Vanessa. It was at the firm's holiday party last year. They didn't look married—they looked like two people acting out what they thought a married couple should be. A performance, not a partnership."

The accuracy of her observation startled Kareem. "You saw that too?"

Fallon nodded. "It was... uncomfortable to watch. Snide little jabs wrapped up in sarcasm, and the two of them avoiding eye contact like it was contagious."

"That's actually a valuable insight," Dr. Harper noted. "Sometimes witnessing the dysfunction in someone else's relationship shines a light on what we refuse to accept in our own."

The conversation lulled for a moment, each processing the implications.

"I'd like to circle back to something you mentioned earlier, Fallon," Dr. Harper said. "You mentioned believing you could have the security of marriage without the vulnerability. That's a big statement. So let me ask you—when you say security, what does that truly mean to you in this moment, in the context of your marriage?"

Fallon considered the question, her legal training evident in her careful formulation of the answer. "I suppose I mean the stability that comes with commitment," she said evenly. "The practical side—shared finances, a certain social image, someone to accompany you to dinners and family functions. The structure, the appearance... without all the messiness."

"And what does that 'messiness' represent to you?"

"Weakness," Fallon said immediately, then caught herself. "Or at least... that's what I was taught to believe growing up. That needing someone—really needing them—meant you were fragile. That if they walked away, everything would fall apart. So you learn not to lean. You stand on your own, even if it's lonely."

"And yet," Dr. Harper observed, gently removing her glasses to make direct eye contact with Fallon, "in trying to protect yourself from emotional vulnerability, you've built a different kind of insecurity in your marriage—one that almost tore it apart. Would you say... that's a fair way to see it?"

Fallon didn't answer immediately, the irony of the situation clearly registering. "I... I never thought of it that way. But yes, I suppose that's right."

Dr. Harper nodded, then glanced at the clock. "We're just about out of time, but before we wrap up, I want to leave you both with something meaningful for the week ahead," she said, her tone calm and intentional. "In relationships where the emotional bond has weakened—where life, stress, and silence have taken up too much space—it can help to treat connection like a muscle. One that needs gentle, intentional work to grow strong again. Think of it like emotional physical therapy... and I want to help you start that healing process."

She reached for a notepad, writing as she spoke. "Here's what I'd like you to try," she said. "Fifteen minutes a day. Just the two of you. No phones, no work talk, no to-do lists. Just heart-to-heart conversation—your feelings, your thoughts, a memory that popped up, something you noticed today."

She looked up, kind but firm. "This isn't about fixing anything. It's about presence. About choosing each other, every single day. That's how connection grows."

Kareem nodded, while Fallon looked skeptical but didn't object.

It's okay if it feels awkward at first—that's completely normal," Dr Harper said, her voice calm and reassuring. "This isn't about getting it perfect. It's about showing up, again and again. Trust isn't built in sweeping moments—it's built in the quiet, everyday choices."

She looked at them both, her gaze full of empathy. "When you spend time together with intention, your stories stay connected—like strands in a rope, stronger together. But if you stop weaving those moments, you start to drift. So let me ask you... can you both commit to giving this a real try, just for this week?"

"Yes," Kareem said.

Fallon hesitated, then nodded. "I can try."

"Excellent." Dr. Harper handed them each a sheet with the exercise outlined. "One last question before we end: What's one thing you each hope to gain from our work together?"

"I want to be seen. Really seen." Kareem said after a moment's reflection. "Not just physically present in the same space, but actually seen and valued for who I am."

Dr. Harper nodded, acknowledging his need without immediately redirecting to Fallon. She let his words have their full weight in the room. Then she turned to Fallon. "And you?"

Fallon studied her hands for a long moment. "What I want... is to know if it's truly possible to be close to someone—*really* close—without disappearing in the process. Without giving up who I am just to keep the peace."

The vulnerability in her admission touched something in Kareem—a reminder of what had drawn him to her in the first place, the strength that could be both barrier and bridge.

"Those are both meaningful goals," Dr. Harper said, replacing her glasses and smiling warmly at both of them. "And here's the beautiful truth—they don't cancel each other out. They actually belong together. You're not searching for someone to fill in your gaps, but someone who honors the fullness of who you already are. Real intimacy doesn't mean losing yourself. It means standing in your truth—and inviting someone in, not to fix you, but to walk with you. So start now. Fifteen minutes."

The conversation loosened slightly after that, moving from the abstract to small personal revelations—Fallon admitting she sometimes felt intimidated by the ease with which others shared their feelings, Kareem acknowledging that his need for connection sometimes masked a fear of abandonment. Nothing earth-shattering, but honest in a way their interactions rarely were.

When the timer chimed, both seemed surprised that the fifteen minutes had passed so quickly.

"That wasn't as terrible as I expected," Fallon admitted

Kareem smirked. "Coming from you, that's practically a standing ovation. Next time, we'll aim for a full smile."

That flicker of playful teasing between them felt like a small green sprout breaking through concrete—delicate, but persistent. A quiet reminder that something alive could still grow where everything once felt empty.

Later that night, as Kareem was answering emails in the spare room they'd converted to a home office, his phone buzzed with a text from Sarah.

Hey you... been a minute. Just checking in—everything good on your end?

He stared at the message, the familiar pull of her warmth and attention momentarily tempting. But it felt different now—more like an echo than a call, a reminder of a path not taken rather than an invitation to follow.

He typed his response carefully:

Things are complicated right now. Fallon and I are working on our marriage. I think it's best if we don't continue our... whatever this was becoming.

Sarah's response came quickly:

I get it. I do. And I respect where you're coming from. Just... know I'll miss our talks. You're a good man, Kareem

And then, a moment later:

If things ever change... you know where to find me

The last message was like a small door left slightly ajar, not quite closed, not quite open. A temptation that would remain available if he chose to revisit it.

Kareem read it twice, then deleted the entire conversation. Some doors were better left not just closed but locked—especially when you were trying to build something that required all your attention elsewhere.

His thoughts were interrupted by a soft knock at the doorway. Fallon stood there, holding two mugs of tea, looking uncharacteristically hesitant.

"I made chamomile," she said, extending one of the mugs toward him. "I remembered you used to drink it before bed."

The small gesture—remembering something about him, making an effort to connect outside their scheduled fifteen minutes—caught Kareem by surprise.

"Thank you," he said, taking the mug. Their fingers brushed briefly, and neither pulled away too quickly.

Fallon paused in the doorway, her tone measured and sincere. "I've been thinking about what Dr. Harper said—about how we've both played a role in the patterns between us." She took a breath, her eyes steady. "I want you to understand that I heard that. And I'm not just showing up for appearances. This matters to me."

The unexpected vulnerability in her admission touched something in Kareem. Not hope, exactly—it was too soon for that—but perhaps its prerequisite, the clearing away of debris that might eventually allow something new to grow.

"I know," he said simply. "Thank you for telling me that."

"We're just now starting to dig below the surface," he added quietly, "but at least we've stopped ignoring the cracks."

Fallon nodded, still standing in the doorway as if uncertain whether to enter or retreat. "Well... goodnight, then."

"Goodnight, Fallon."

As she turned to go, Kareem found himself thinking about Dr. Harper's observation that true intimacy wasn't about erasing boundaries but about choosing to share ourselves across them. It was too early to tell if they could rebuild what had been damaged, but for the first time in years, he felt the faint outline of a bridge beginning to form between them—tentative, fragile, but real.

Whether it could truly hold the weight of everything they'd been through—that was still uncertain. But for the first time, they were both looking at the distance between them, not pretending it wasn't there. And that mattered. Because healing didn't begin with answers—it began with honesty. And crossing that space would take more than hope. It would take effort. Intention. Heart. From *both* of them.

Chapter Nine

Landmines

The Shaws' dining room was a study in luxury—all clean lines and neutral tones, the kind of space that appeared in architectural magazines. Their dinner parties were equally curated, with guests selected for professional compatibility and conversation steered toward accomplishments rather than feelings. Devon and Vanessa Shaw had been throwing these kinds of dinners for years, and Kareem and Fallon were regulars, along with two other couples from Devon's job. Everyone was successful, dressed to impress, and playing the part of close friends—even if some of it felt a little fake.

Tonight's dinner was supposed to celebrate Kareem's promotion to senior financial analyst. But as Kareem watched Devon laughing and talking at the head of the table with a drink in his hand, he started to wonder if the night was really about him—or if it was more about Devon showing everyone he was still the center of attention.

“So when are they gonna let you touch the big boy money?” Devon asked, refilling Kareem's wine glass without waiting for permission. "Or you still back there doing math for folks who already rich?"

"It’s actually a pretty major move," Kareem replied. "I’ll be leading the team on the Meridian acquisition. This time, I’m not just running numbers—I’m structuring the deal. Calling shots from our side of the table."

"Well, look at *you*," Devon grinned, raising his glass in a toast that somehow managed to feel both congratulatory and condescending. "Moving on up in the world. Just remember us little people when you start signing them million-dollar checks." He raised his glass with a grin that didn't quite reach his eyes.

Vanessa, elegant in a fitted black dress that spoke of careful maintenance, offered a tight smile from the other end of the table. "How wonderful for you both," she said, her smile perfectly calibrated. "It must be such a relief, Fallon, to finally have some... balance in the partnership."

The comment landed like a small grenade at the table—not quite an explosion, but a moment where everyone tensed, waiting to see if the situation would escalate. Kareem looked across the table at Fallon, wondering how she'd handle the not-so-subtle jab.

Fallon took a measured sip of her wine, her expression unreadable. "Kareem's always brought a certain brilliance to his work," she said evenly. "It's gratifying to see the firm finally catching up to that."

The words were right, Kareem thought, but something in her tone felt off—like she was giving testimony she didn't quite believe. Still, it was more supportive than he had expected, given the fragile state of their relationship over the past two weeks.

Since beginning therapy with Dr. Harper, they had maintained their daily fifteen minutes of connection with surprising consistency. Sometimes awkward, sometimes surprisingly intimate, the conversations had created a thin bridge between them. But even the strongest bridges can buckle under pressure, and Kareem knew all too well how much hurt still lingered beneath the surface of their relationship—unspoken, unresolved, and waiting to crack.

"Man, don't start walking around like you God's gift to finance," Devon said with a laugh, turning to Greg Bowden, one of his law firm colleagues. "Remember when Cameron made partner? That fool went out and bought a Tesla the next morning—like Jesus handed him the keys himself! Acting like he just parted the Red Sea with a spreadsheet!"

The conversation shifted, and Kareem felt himself relax slightly, grateful for Devon's short attention span. Across the table, Fallon was talking with Regina Bowden about a recent court decision. Her focus was intense, just like it always was when she talked about the law. Watching her, Kareem was reminded of what had first drawn him to her—that fierce intelligence, the precision of her mind, the way she commanded attention without seeking it.

"And how are things with you two?" Vanessa asked quietly, having moved to the empty chair beside him while Devon held court at the other end of the table. "Devon said you guys have been going through some... changes."

Kareem bristled at the thought of Devon discussing their marital problems. "We're working through some things," he said carefully. "But we're good."

Vanessa's smile didn't reach her eyes. "Marriage is a marathon, not a sprint," she said, her voice carrying the particular weariness of someone who had been running for too long. "And sometimes... you realize you're not even running the same race."

Before Kareem could respond, Devon tapped his glass with a knife, the sharp ping drawing everyone's attention. "Alright now, since we all here acting fancy for Kareem's big-time promotion," Devon announced. "Let's raise a glass to my boy finally making it to the big leagues." He held up his drink, "To Kareem. To finally getting his piece of the pie. About time somebody recognized what we've all known for years. He paused, smile widening. "Of course, Fallon's been carrying the financial load so long, she probably forgot what it's like to have help."

Uncomfortable laughter rippled around the table as Devon continued, his smile wide but his eyes calculating.

"Seriously though, I've known this man since dinosaurs roamed the Earth. Kareem always been the dependable one—steady, solid, doing' things the right way, by the Lord's instruction manual. You know, the type who pay bills early and actually read the terms and conditions."

He lifted his glass even higher now, "So here's to Kareem!"

"And let's not forget Fallon," Devon added, his gaze shifting to her with subtle challenge. Must be real nice... having your man finally start catching up just a *little bit,* huh?"

The comment hung in the air like bait. Kareem watched Fallon, suddenly tense, wondering how she would navigate it.

Fallon smiled her practiced courtroom smile. "I think ambition looks different for different people," she said diplomatically. "Kareem's promotion is exactly what it should be: a thoughtful acknowledgment of his hard work and remarkable ability."

Then she continued, seemingly unable to help herself.

"Of course, in finance, titles do tend to fly around a bit more freely than they do in law. Senior analyst is certainly admirable—but let's not pretend it's the same as making partner at a top-tier firm" She sipped her wine casually. "Apples and oranges, darling."

The room went quiet. Everyone else suddenly looked down at their dessert plates, pretending to be interested. Kareem felt a cold heaviness settle inside him—the feeling of being embarrassed in front of everyone by the one person he wanted approval from the most.

Fallon seemed to realize her mistake almost immediately. Her eyes widened slightly, and she set down her wine glass with careful precision. "What I meant to say is—that's precisely why Kareem's success is so meaningful. He's thriving in a space that still respects integrity. Where quiet excellence speaks louder than flash, and substance outshines strategy."

It was too late. The damage was done. Kareem offered a tight smile, raising his glass slightly in acknowledgment before taking a long drink, using the motion to mask whatever might be visible in his eyes.

The conversation mercifully moved on, turning to safer topics—the latest restaurant openings, someone's upcoming vacation to Portugal, a debate about a new Netflix series. Kareem moved through the motions on autopilot, saying all the right things while something inside him shifted. The pain, once sharp and aching, began to settle—no longer bleeding, just hardening. Cooling. Turning into something colder, quieter, and far more difficult to reach.

By the time farewells were exchanged, the evening had slipped back into its polished facade. Devon gave Kareem a hearty clap on the shoulder, all grins, vowing to arrange a golf outing "soon." Vanessa offered Fallon an air-kiss and a vague mention of lunch plans neither of them intended to keep. And then, just like that, Kareem and Fallon were alone in their car—surrounded by silence so thick, it practically vibrated with everything they weren't saying.

Fallon was the first to break it, her voice carefully controlled. "I'm sorry about what I said back there."

Kareem kept his eyes on the road. "Which part?"

"You know which part." She sighed, staring out the passenger window at the passing streetlights. "The comment about your promotion versus making partner. It was... unnecessary."

“Unnecessary,” Kareem echoed, his voice low and measured. “Not out of line. Not disrespectful. Just... unnecessary.” He shook his head, eyes still on the road. “That’s what we’re calling it now?”

"That's not what I meant."

"Then what did you mean, Fallon? Because the way it came out? It sounded like you wanted to remind everybody that you’re still ahead. That no matter what I do, how hard I work... I’m still playing catch-up.”

Fallon turned toward him, her expression frustrated. “That’s not fair, Kareem. I was doing my best to rise above Devon’s little game. You know how he is—always looking for a reaction.”

“And he did what he set out to do,” he said, low and firm. “'Cause instead of just saying you were proud of me... you had to add the asterisk. Had to let the whole room know—let *me* know—where I stand. Remind me there's still a ladder.”

"I was proud of you," Fallon insisted. "I am proud of you."

"Just not as proud as you are of yourself."

His words lingered in the air—sharper than he meant, but no less true for it. Fallon didn't respond. She simply turned back to the window, her profile calm but distant. The rest of the drive passed in silence, each mile thick with everything they couldn't—or wouldn't—say.

Later that night, after they'd changed clothes and gone through their quiet, separate bedtime rituals, Kareem stepped into the bedroom to find Fallon perched at the edge of the bed. She was still awake, despite the hour, her posture composed but her face—unguarded. Soft in a way he rarely saw, as if the armor had slipped without her noticing.

"I need to say something," she said, her voice quiet but steady. "“And I need you to truly listen—not to react, not to defend, but to understand—before you say anything back."

Kareem hesitated in the doorway, part of him still raw from the earlier hurt, another part recognizing the vulnerability in her posture. After a moment, he nodded and moved to sit beside her, leaving enough space between them for comfort.

Fallon began, staring down at her hands, “What happened tonight,” she said evenly, “was me slipping into an old habit—one I know too well. It’s that instinct to protect myself by creating distance. To make sure I’m the one holding the power, the status... the upper hand.” She lifted her head, meeting his eyes without flinching. “If Dr. Harper were here, she’d probably call it what it is—me rebuilding that emotional fortress we’ve been working so hard to dismantle.”

Kareem remained silent, sensing she wasn't finished.

"Kareem, let me be clear. I am proud of you. Unapologetically proud. Watching you grow, watching you lead—it’s a beautiful thing.” She paused, her eyes softening, but her words stayed deliberate. “And yet... I’d be lying if I said that pride didn’t come tangled with something else. Something a little more complicated. Perhaps even... threatened.”

The admission seemed difficult for her, the words coming out carefully measured. "When you outgrow the box I've put you in, it challenges the story I've been telling myself about why I need to keep my guard up."

"What story is that?" Kareem asked quietly.

Fallon's laugh was small, brittle. "That you need me more than I need you. That I'm the successful one, the driven one, so it's okay for me to withhold parts of myself because you... you won't leave." She shook her head, the vulnerability in her expression painful to witness. "It's ugly to say out loud. But it's the truth."

The honesty caught him off guard. In seven years of marriage, Fallon had never opened up like this about what was going on inside her. It was like their sessions with Dr. Harper had given her the words she never had before—a way to dig deep and explain things she used to cover up with excuses and careful logic.

“I don’t know if I can trust that you won’t shut me out again,” Kareem said after a long moment. “Yeah, we’re doing the therapy. We’re having the talks. But when life gets hard—when the pressure’s on—how do I know you won’t go right back behind those walls?”

"You don't," Fallon replied simply. "And the truth is... I don't know if I can be what you need." Her voice caught slightly. "I don't know if I can open myself up enough—be vulnerable enough—to give you the kind of emotional intimacy you're asking for. I want to. I'm trying. But some days... I wonder if I even know how."

The confession sat between them, heavy and honest. It hurt to say, but it also felt like a small release. There were no promises, no comforting lies—just the raw truth that neither of them knew what would happen next.

"So where does that leave us?" Kareem asked.

Fallon was quiet for a moment. "I don't know," she said finally. "But I want to keep trying. If you do."

Kareem watched her carefully, as if looking for that polished, put-together version of Fallon who had downplayed his success just hours ago. But that woman wasn't in front of him now. No, what he saw was something far more rare. Fallon—without the mask, without the sharp edges. She was tired, yes. Unsure. But she was also fully present, showing a kind of honesty she usually kept locked away. And in that moment, Kareem saw not just his wife—but the woman beneath all the layers, finally letting herself be seen.

"I want to keep trying too," he said. And despite everything, he meant it.

The news came on a Tuesday morning conference call that Kareem expected to be routine—budget reviews, timeline updates, the usual. Then it landed, almost like an afterthought: Chicago. Two weeks. A senior-level team was heading out to finalize the Meridian acquisition—the very deal Kareem had been promoted to lead, the one meant to solidify his reputation. It wasn't until the call was ending that Richard Manley, the head of their division, mentioned the composition of the team.

"We'll need Thomas from Legal, Andrews from Risk, you, obviously, and we're coordinating with Apex's marketing team for the brand valuation portion," Manley said. "They're sending Sarah Winters as their lead."

Kareem felt a cold knot form in his stomach. "Sarah Winters?" he repeated, struggling to keep his voice neutral.

"Yes, apparently she's their new Director of Brand Strategy. You know her?"

"We went to college together," Kareem said, his tone deliberately casual. "Small world."

"Well, that's convenient," Manley replied. "Always helpful to have some rapport established. Their CEO speaks highly of her work."

As he ended the call, Kareem sat motionless at his desk, staring at the blank screen of his phone. Two weeks in Chicago with Sarah. Two weeks of working closely with the woman he had nearly betrayed his marriage for, just as he and Fallon were beginning to rebuild their fragile connection.

The prep meeting should have been straightforward—two firms, neutral territory, professional coordination. Instead, Kareem found himself acutely aware of Sarah across the conference table, her presence shifting the entire dynamic of the room. She wore a sharp navy blazer, every bit the polished professional. But when their eyes met—just for a second—there was something there. And even though Kareem had drawn the line, even though the boundary was clear, that look carried the weight of what once was—and what could have been, if life had unfolded differently.

"Ellis & Dean will lead on the financial modeling," Manley was saying. "Apex will handle the brand integration presentation."

Sarah nodded, her gaze flicking to Kareem. "We should probably sync up on the valuation projections," she said, her voice professionally neutral but with a warmth underneath that only he would notice. "I'll need your team's numbers to finalize the marketing forecasts."

"Of course," Kareem responded, keeping his tone equally professional. "I'll make sure you have everything you need."

After the meeting, as they gathered their materials, she paused beside him. "Chicago," she said softly, tilting her head with a knowing smile. "Never thought we'd find our way back here." Then, with a playful wink, she added, "But here we are."

"Sarah—"

"Don't worry," she interrupted with a small smile. "I understand the boundaries. But two weeks is a long time." She smoothed a hand over her short curls—an old habit he hadn't realized he missed. "A lot can happen. People change... sometimes even their minds."

Before Kareem could say a word, she was already gone. And just like that, he was left standing there, feeling the weight of what was really ahead. That trip to Chicago wasn't just about work—it was going to test his loyalty, his focus, and whether he was truly ready to fight for the fragile thing he and Fallon were trying to piece back together.

The old Kareem would have called Devon immediately—seeking that familiar voice that made complicated situations feel manageable, even when the advice wasn't sound. Kareem even pulled up his number, ready to reach out. His thumb hovered over the call button—hesitating, unsure if this was the moment to bring someone else into something so personal.

Then he paused, remembering Dr. Harper's question: *Has Devon's approach to his marriage—finding connection outside rather than addressing issues within—brought him peace? Has it made him truly happy?*

The truth was right there, plain as day, in the way Devon and Vanessa had acted at dinner.That wasn't what Kareem wanted for himself, for his marriage. He put down the phone without making the call. Devon's advice, however well-intentioned, would come from a place of compromise rather than courage. And right now, he needed something stronger than that. He needed courage—the kind that tells the truth, even when it's uncomfortable. The kind that faces problems directly instead of hiding from them.

Instead, he texted Fallon: *Need to talk tonight. Nothing wrong, but something important came up at work.*

Her response came quickly: *OK. Dinner at home? I can be there by 7.*

Perfect. I'll cook.

From the outside, it seemed like a simple moment. But underneath, it held so much more. Kareem sat back down at his desk, a quiet sense of peace settling over him. He knew the road ahead wouldn't be easy. But one thing was clear—he was making a different choice than the one Devon had shown him. He was choosing truth, even when it was hard, instead of hiding behind a lie that felt safe.

That evening, as they sat across from each other at their kitchen table, the remains of a simple pasta dinner between them, Kareem explained the situation. He watched Fallon's face carefully as he spoke, noting the subtle shifts in her expression as she processed what he was telling her.

"So you'll be in Chicago for two weeks," she said when he had finished. "Working directly with Sarah." She took a sip of her water, her face composed but her knuckles white around the glass. "And when, exactly, do you leave?"

"Monday morning," Kareem replied. "Manley wants us there for their executive team meeting."

Fallon gave a composed nod, her movements measured as she placed her glass gently on the table. Her voice was calm, gracious, and unmistakably clear. "Thank you for sharing that with me. I appreciate your honesty."

"I wouldn't keep something like this from you," Kareem said. "Not after everything we've been fighting through, everything we've been trying to rebuild.

Fallon was quiet for a moment, her gaze fixed on some middle distance. "What would you have done a month ago?" she asked suddenly. "Before therapy, before our confrontation. Would you have told me then?"

The question caught Kareem off guard with its directness. "I... I don't know," he admitted. "Maybe not. Or maybe I would have mentioned the trip but not specifically who was going."

"And now?"

"Now I'm trying to be fully transparent. Even when it's uncomfortable."

Fallon nodded slowly, absorbing this. "Have you told her? About us working on things?"

"Not yet," Kareem said. "I haven't spoken to her directly since I ended our... whatever it was."

"But you will see her before the trip," Fallon said, not quite a question.

"There's a team meeting on Friday to prepare," Kareem confirmed. "She'll be there."

Fallon's jaw tightened almost imperceptibly. "And you want to go? On this trip?"

"Yeah, it's a big opportunity," Kareem said carefully. "The kind most people pray for and never get. But that's not the whole point. I don't want to run from difficult situations anymore. That's what got us into this mess in the first place—avoiding what was hard instead of facing it."

Fallon was silent for several long moments, her expression unreadable. When she finally spoke, her voice was quiet but steady.

"I'm scared you'll be with her," she said, the admission visibly difficult for her. "The thought of you spending two weeks in another city with her—late nights, dinners, drinks—it unsettles me more than I'd like to admit." She trailed off, then met his eyes directly. "But I'm choosing to trust you," she said, the words deliberate. "Not because I'm not afraid, but because the alternative, living in constant fear, would destroy what we're trying to build."

The sincerity in her voice landed with quiet force, settling in Kareem's chest like truth long overdue. Just weeks ago, Fallon would've met this moment with polished restraint—cool, measured, untouchable. It was her way of keeping pain at a distance, of convincing herself that detachment was strength. But now, here she was—unshielded, naming her fear without turning it into a weapon. It was unfamiliar ground for both of them, and all the more powerful because of it.

"That means a lot to me," he said simply. "And I won't betray that trust."

Fallon nodded, then rose to clear their plates, the familiar routine offering a moment's respite from the emotional intensity of their conversation. As she loaded the dishwasher, every motion calm and deliberate, she kept her eyes on the task in front of her, speaking without looking his way.

"Will you let me know when you arrive? And maybe... check in sometimes while you're there?"

"Of course," Kareem said. "Every day, if you want."

Fallon closed the dishwasher and turned to face him, leaning against the counter. "I'd like that."

Something shifted between them in that moment—a small but significant realignment. Fallon asking for reassurance rather than demanding it or pretending not to need it. Kareem offering connection rather than waiting for permission to provide it.

Dr. Harper would probably call it progress, Kareem thought. But progress wasn't a straight line. It was a series of steps forward and back, navigating around the landmines of old patterns and unhealed wounds, each of them trying not to trigger an explosion that could undo what they were so carefully rebuilding.

Monday morning arrived with the familiar urgency that only travel days seem to bring. Kareem moved through the house with quiet efficiency—gathering the last of his things, reviewing his itinerary, confirming his ride to the airport. Fallon had already slipped out for an early court appearance, their goodbye unfolding in the muted stillness of pre-dawn. It had been brief—slightly awkward, yet unmistakably sincere. And just before she walked out the door, she'd done something unexpected: she hugged him. Not out of habit, but intention. And in that small, quiet gesture, something unspoken passed between them.

In the back of the Lyft, Kareem scrolled through work emails, answering the most urgent ones and flagging others for later attention. The Chicago trip loomed before him, a complex mixture of professional opportunity and personal challenge. He was still absorbing the reality of it when his phone buzzed with a text from Fallon.

Good luck today. Safe travels. Let me know when you land.

They were simple words—nothing extravagant, the kind couples trade without a second thought. But coming from Fallon, they meant far more. They signaled intention. A decision not to retreat behind silence, but to step forward. To acknowledge the bond between them rather than pretend it didn't matter. Kareem sat there, phone in hand, the weight of her message settling in. He hadn't yet found the right words to reply when another message lit up the screen.

I love you.

Three simple words—words that had become almost routine in their marriage, spoken more out of habit than heartfelt intention. But here, in this moment, stripped of pretense and filled with quiet vulnerability, they landed differently. There was no performance, no obligation—just honesty, however uncertain. And that sincerity disarmed Kareem, catching him off guard. He felt a tightness rise in his throat as he reached for his phone, choosing his response with the same care the moment deserved.

I love you too. Talk tonight.

The airport buzzed with the familiar chaos of departure—hurried footsteps, rolling luggage, the constant hum of announcements. Kareem moved through it automatically, his mind split between the professional opportunity ahead and the fragile trust he was carrying with him.

Boarding pass scanned. Security cleared. Gate found. The well-rehearsed rhythm of travel moved Kareem along without effort, each step a quiet distraction from the weight he carried. He took his seat as the flight attendant's voice calmly reminded passengers to switch their devices to airplane mode. He glanced at his phone one last time. Fallon's message—simple, unexpected—sat there like an open door: I love you. A moment later, the cabin door closed with a firm, final sound. Kareem powered down his phone, severing the line between what he was leaving behind and what lay ahead. The engines roared to life, lifting him toward Chicago, toward Sarah, and into the uncertainty of choices not yet made.

Chapter Ten

Testing Grounds

Chicago greeted Kareem with sharp wind and gray skies that hadn't quite released winter's grip. From the airplane window, the city stretched wide and determined below him: a tapestry of ambition, grit, and legacy. Fitting, he thought, for the challenge that lay ahead.

Meridian's headquarters rose in glass and steel above the city, Lake Michigan stretching beyond its boardroom windows. The morning unfolded in swift succession: names exchanged, hands shaken, smiles practiced. This was the opening act of a corporate courtship, and Kareem played his part with composed precision. When it came time to present his financial projections, he spoke with assurance, answering questions with the measured authority his title now demanded.

Sarah sat across from him, her laptop open, occasionally jotting down notes with quiet focus. She wore a tailored burgundy dress—elegant, understated, yet impossible to ignore. Her makeup was subtle except for the bold lip color that drew attention to her smile. After lunch, when she rose to present the Apex brand strategy, the shift was immediate. The room quieted, attentive. She didn't demand the floor—she owned it. With the same effortless command Kareem had seen in their college days, Sarah spoke with clarity, presence, and that undeniable spark that made people lean in

"The Meridian acquisition isn't just about adding to our portfolio," Sarah said smoothly, her voice calm but confident. Her slides backed her up with clean, compelling numbers that lined up perfectly with Kareem's projections. "It's about honoring the story Meridian's already told—preserving that brand legacy—while weaving it seamlessly into the bigger picture of Ellis & Dean. One story, stronger together."

Kareem nodded thoughtfully, a quiet admiration settling in. Her strategic mind was as sharp as ever, and he couldn't help but respect that. Whatever history lay between them personally, it hadn't dulled their professional rhythm—in fact, it may have refined it. There was an ease in their communication now, a practiced efficiency born from familiarity that kept the day's meetings focused and productive.

It was only later, in the elevator down to the lobby, that the professional exterior showed its first crack.

"Dinner plans?" Sarah asked, her tone light but laced with curiosity, as the elevator doors closed around them, sealing them into the quiet tension of the ride down.

"Turning in early," Kareem said with a smooth grin, adjusting his cuff like it was part of the performance. "Got a date with some counter-offers in the morning—thrilling stuff, I know."

Sarah smiled, slow and warm, her eyes lingering on him a little longer than necessary. "Always the thorough one," she said. "Guess some things... don't change after all."

Kareem maintained eye contact, his response measured. "Some things shouldn't."

The elevator doors slid open onto the polished marble lobby, bringing a quiet end to the moment. But something had shifted—an understanding had been set in place. Unspoken, yet unmistakably firm. As they stepped outside and went their separate ways—Sarah offering a graceful wave, Kareem returning it with a courteous nod—he knew the first test had come and gone. And while he wasn't entirely sure he had passed, he had at least chosen to take it with integrity.

In his hotel room that night, Kareem set up his laptop for the call with Fallon, the desk lamp casting shadows that made him look more tired than he felt. When Fallon appeared on screen—hair still styled from court, makeup faded—the awkwardness between them was immediate.

"How was the flight?" she asked, her tone formal, as if speaking to a business associate rather than her husband.

"On time, surprisingly," Kareem replied, equally stilted. "How was court?"

"Motion granted. Judge Watkins was actually reasonable for once."

They carried on for a few more minutes, trading updates as if checking boxes rather than truly engaging. The words filled the space, but not the distance. Then the conversation settled into a quiet stillness—awkward, unspoken. Kareem looked at Fallon's face on the screen, so familiar and yet oddly removed. It felt less like speaking to his wife and more like gazing at an old portrait—someone he once knew intimately, now blurred by time and silence.

"This is weird... right?" he finally said.

Fallon's laugh was small but genuine. "Extremely."

"We're sitting' here talking like strangers," Kareem observed.

"We've been strangers for a while now," Fallon replied, the honesty catching him off guard. "Maybe that's why this feels so unfamiliar."

The truth of the moment settled between them, uncomfortable but true. Then Fallon surprised him.

"I'm seeing my parents this weekend," she said. "Separately, obviously. Putting them in the same room is like tossing a match in a gas leak"

Kareem raised his eyebrows, genuinely surprised. "Your parents? You haven't seen them in what—two years?"

"Three." Fallon's expression was unreadable. "My mother at least. I saw my father at a cousin's wedding last year, but we barely spoke."

“What made you do that?” Kareem asked carefully.

Fallon was quiet for a moment. “Dr. Harper suggested it might offer some clarity,” she said evenly. “To revisit how their divorce may have influenced the way I see relationships” Her gaze shifted, just for a moment, then returned with quiet resolve. “She believes I may be repeating patterns I’ve never taken the time to truly examine.”

"And you agree?" Kareem couldn't keep the surprise from his voice. The Fallon he knew would have dismissed such a suggestion as psychological oversimplification.

“I’m not entirely sure,” Fallon admitted. "But I'm tired of being afraid all the time."

"Afraid of what?"

"Of becoming my mother," she said simply. "Falling head over heels, giving everything, then watching it all go up in flames."

The honesty in her words stopped Kareem in his tracks. In all their years together, he had never heard Fallon speak with such unguarded clarity. And in that moment, he realized he was witnessing something rare: Fallon, not as the accomplished attorney or the composed wife, but as a woman laying bare the fear she had tried so long to outthink.

"I'm proud of you," he said finally. "That takes courage."

"We'll see," Fallon replied, but there was a softness to her skepticism that was new. "How are things there? With... the team?"

Kareem recognized the carefully phrased question for what it was. "Strictly professional," he answered. "Sarah is very good at what she does. The presentations went well."

Fallon nodded, absorbing this. "And outside of the presentations?"

"There was a moment... in the elevator," Kareem said, steady and direct. "Wasn't anything said, wasn't anything done—but I felt it. You know? That shift in the air." He looked her dead in the eye. "But I shut it down. Made it real clear—there's a line, and I'm not crossing it."

"Thank you," Fallon said quietly. "For telling me."

Another silence fell, but this one felt different—not strained but thoughtful. Something had shifted, some small measure of trust rebuilt through this exchange of truths.

"You're welcome. Unfortunately, I have some work to do. We can do this again tomorrow? Same time?" Kareem asked.

"I'd like that," Fallon replied.

As the call ended, Kareem sat back in his hotel chair, struck by the strangeness of it all. Somehow, with three thousand miles between them, they had managed a level of honesty that had eluded them across their own dining table for years.

The next morning, Kareem's phone buzzed with a text as he was preparing for the day's meetings.

How's Chicago treating you? More importantly... how Sarah treating you? Don't front now.

Devon's message had its usual mix of joking around and hidden jabs. Kareem looked at it for a while, thinking hard about what to say back. He knew his reply needed to count.

Professional and focused, which is what this trip needs to be.

Devon's reply came quickly:

Come on man, no one's saying wreck your marriage. I'm just saying what happens in the Chi? Stays in the Chi...

Kareem felt the usual pull—the way Devon always seemed to offer a sense of friendship, the easy way out, and the permission to relax. But this time, Kareem saw something deeper: Devon wasn't just looking for a good time; he was trying to make his own choices feel right by getting others to do the same.

No I'm good. Working on making things right with Fallon.

There was a longer pause before Devon's next message appeared:

Hey man it's your call. But life too short for all that working out. Now I don't know if you're tougher than me or if you just ain't learned how the game really go yet. But either way, handle your business at them meetings, man. Good luck to ya!

The message lingered in Kareem's mind as he went through his day, dealing with the business talks. Devon's words said more about how he was feeling than he probably meant. Underneath all that tough talk was a sense of doubt—a little hint of regret that Devon might not even realize he was showing.

By Thursday evening, the acquisition talks had reached a turning point. The numbers were finally in sync, but there were still arguments about how to merge the staff and who would be in charge. The tension in the conference room had been building all afternoon. When Richard Manley finally spoke, everyone knew it was time to pause and rethink the plan.

"Let's pick this up tomorrow after everyone's had time to review the revised terms," he announced, closing his leather portfolio with finality. "Team dinner at Gibson's, seven o'clock. We'll talk strategy in a more relaxed setting."

As the room emptied, Sarah lingered, organizing her presentation materials with deliberate slowness until she and Kareem were the last ones present.

"Gibson's has the best steaks in Chicago," she said, not looking up from her papers. "But trust me, it's the Old Fashioneds that really keep me coming back."

"I've heard that," Kareem replied neutrally.

Sarah finally met his eyes. "How about we grab a drink before the others show up? Maybe around six? You know, for old times' sake."

The invitation lingered between them, seeming professional but with a hint of something more personal. Kareem could feel the tension in the air—this was the first real challenge to his decision.

"I appreciate the offer," he said carefully, "but I've got a video call scheduled with Fallon at six."

Something flickered in Sarah's expression—disappointment, perhaps, or a reassessment. "Of course," she said smoothly. "Another time."

But they both knew there wouldn't be another time. A boundary had been established, not with awkwardness or drama, but with the simple prioritization of his marriage over convenience or temptation.

Fallon's Saturday lunch with her mother took place at the fancy Langham Hotel's restaurant—a place her mother picked, of course. At sixty-two, Diana Miller still commanded attention—perfectly styled hair, subtle makeup, clothes chosen for impression rather than comfort. Everything about her suggested someone who had learned to measure worth through appearance.

"Fallon, it's been too long," she greeted Fallon with air kisses that wouldn't disturb either of their makeup. You look a little tired, honey. You getting enough rest?

I always told you, preventative skincare starts in your twenties, darling."

"It's good to see you too, Mom," Fallon replied, already feeling the familiar tension settling between her shoulder blades.

The first half hour went by like it always did—her mother asking gentle but pointed questions about Fallon's job, dropping little criticisms that she pretended were just concern. She told stories about other people's children who weren't doing well enough. Fallon answered carefully, giving just enough detail to keep her mother happy without really sharing anything important.

It wasn't until their entrées arrived that Fallon steered the conversation toward her actual purpose.

"Mom, there's something I've been meaning to ask you... about when Dad left."

Diana's fork paused halfway to her mouth, her expression freezing momentarily before she recovered. "Really, Fallon? Do we have to go there? That was decades ago."

"I need to understand something," Fallon pressed on. "After he left—the person you became—that wasn't the mother I knew before."

"Honey, folks change once they've been hurt," Diana said, her voice heavy with meaning. "Now, I know with all that fancy lawyering you do, you've seen enough to know that's true."

"You fell apart," Fallon said quietly. "I was twelve, and suddenly I was the adult in the house."

Diana set down her fork with deliberate control. "Is this why you wanted to see me? To criticize my parenting during the most difficult time of my life?"

"No," Fallon said, maintaining her composure. "I'm trying to understand how it shaped me. How watching you suffer like that affected the way I approach my own marriage."

Something in Diana's expression shifted—surprise, perhaps, at this unexpected vulnerability from her typically guarded daughter.

"Your marriage? Are you and Kareem having problems?"

Fallon took a deep breath. "We're working through some things. And I'm realizing that I've built walls to protect myself from the kind of pain I watched you go through. But those walls—they're keeping Kareem out too."

Diana was quiet for a long moment, studying Fallon with new attention. When she finally spoke, her voice had lost its defensive edge.

"After your daddy left, baby, I swear I thought I was gonna die from the hurt," she said, her voice soft but heavy with truth. "And I'm not talking figuratively, honey—I really thought my heart was just gonna stop. I had wrapped up everything about me in him, in the family we built together. When he walked out that door, I didn't know who I was supposed to be anymore."

Fallon felt her throat tighten. "I remember."

Diana leaned back, her eyes softening as she found the right words. "Baby, what you probably don't know," she began, voice warm and honest, "is that I was the one who drove him away. I swear it wasn't my intention, but that's exactly what happened." She paused, looking out the window as if the answer lay beyond the glass. "I was so terrified of losing him that I clung on too tight—I tracked his every move, questioned every friend he had, needed him to tell me over and over that he wasn't going anywhere. Before I knew it, the love I was trying so hard to save became the very prison he felt he had to escape."

The admission stunned Fallon. In all the years since the divorce, her mother had never acknowledged any responsibility, had always positioned herself solely as the victim of her father's selfishness.

"I didn't know that," Fallon said quietly.

"How could you know? You were just a child, and me? I... I wasn't well." Diana reached across the table, a rare move for her. "But listen, Fallon, the mistake I made wasn't loving your father too much. No, baby, it was loving myself too little. I didn't know who I was outside of being his wife, being your mother. When he walked out, I realized there was nothing left of me."

Fallon felt like the wind had been knocked out of her. "So you think I've done the opposite? That I've built my identity so far apart from Kareem that there's no space left for a real connection?"

"Haven't you?" Diana asked simply.

The question lingered between them as their lunch progressed, remaining present even as they moved on to lighter conversation. By the time they said their goodbyes on the sidewalk outside the hotel, something subtle yet meaningful had changed—not exactly a resolution, but certainly a fresh understanding Fallon would carry forward into her day.

Her father's Streeterville apartment revealed his engineer's mind—functional furniture, minimal decoration, everything in its place. Richard Miller had remarried and divorced again since leaving her mother, but the space showed no traces of either relationship.

"You want something to drink?" he offered as Fallon settled onto his leather sofa. "Got some water... coffee too. Might even be a little wine tucked away somewhere, if you're feeling' fancy."

"Water is fine," Fallon replied, watching him move to the kitchen with the slight stiffness that came with age. He had always been tall and lean, but the years had begun to curve his shoulders, silver now dominating his once-dark hair.

He came back with two glasses of water and sat across from her in a chair that looked like it was picked more for comfort than looks. The awkward feeling between them was nothing new—it was the kind of quiet space that happens when two people are family, but haven't really shared their feelings in a long, long time

"Your mother said you visited her today," he said, surprising Fallon. "She gave me a call."

"You two are speaking again?" Fallon couldn't hide her shock.

Richard smiled slightly. "Every now and then. Mostly about you or your brother. Sometimes about grandchildren we don't yet have." He shrugged. "Time... well, it has a way of softening even the sharpest edges."

"She told me something interesting," Fallon said, deciding to take a direct approach. "She said she drove you away by clinging too tightly."

Her father's eyebrows rose. "Diana said that? Well now... that's unexpected."

""Is it true?"

"Partially," he said at last, his voice calm and steady. "Your mother was... focused. She held on tight to what we had, tried to shape it into what she believed it should be. But no, that's not why I left."

"Why did you, then?" Fallon asked, the question she had wanted to ask for twenty years finally finding voice.

"Because I was a coward," he said, his voice low and steady. "There were problems—real ones. Your mother's anxiety. My own way of shutting down. We were living two different stories, under the same roof. But the truth is, I never really tried to fix it." He looked Fallon straight in the eyes. "I didn't fight for your mother when it mattered most. I took the easy road—a fresh start, a new chapter—because I was too afraid to face the hard work of healing what we had."

The admission landed like a physical weight on Fallon's chest. "You could have tried harder," she said, her voice tight with old pain.

"Yes," her father agreed without defensiveness. "I absolutely could have. Should have." He leaned forward, his expression serious. "Is that why you're here, Fallon? Because you're at that crossroads yourself?"

Fallon looked away, uncomfortable with his perception. "Kareem and I are having some issues," she admitted. "We're in therapy."

"That's more than your mother and I ever did," Richard observed. "Takes a fair amount of courage to do what you're doing."

"It's complicated," Fallon said. "I've kept him at a distance emotionally. Built walls to protect myself. And now he's..." She hesitated. "He's in Chicago on business, working with an ex. Someone he nearly had an affair with."

She expected judgment or dismissal from her father. Instead, he was quiet for a long moment, considering her words with unexpected thoughtfulness.

"You know what I've learned, Fallon? Running away... now that's the easy part. But staying—facing the mess, doing the work—that takes real strength." He paused, shaking his head with the weight of memory. "Took me two broken marriages to understand that. So when I see you trying to do better... trying not to repeat what I did... I respect that. I truly do."

"I don't know if it's enough," Fallon admitted. "If I can be what he needs."

"Maybe it's not about being what he needs," Richard suggested. "Maybe it's about being yourself—fully, honestly—and seeing if that person and who he truly is can build something worth keeping."

The simplicity of this perspective caught Fallon off guard. Her father had never been one for emotional wisdom, had always approached problems with engineer's logic rather than psychological insight. Yet here, in his apartment with its view of the city they both loved, he had offered her something unexpected—not absolution for his past mistakes, but a perspective forged from their consequences.

The team dinner at Gibson's had that familiar energy of business blending with pleasure—connections strengthening over wine, alliances forming between courses. Kareem had chosen his seat with intention—close enough to contribute, but not the center of attention. He engaged in conversation thoughtfully, always keeping one eye on the clock. Across the table, just slightly diagonal, sat Sarah. She was animated, confidently discussing Apex's brand refresh with a Meridian executive. Every so often, her eyes would meet Kareem's. A look that said more than words ever could.

At 8:30, Kareem discreetly checked his watch, then stood, making his excuses to Manley. "I need to step out for a scheduled call with my team back home," he explained, the half-truth smooth on his lips. "Don't stop the show on my account. Handle your business."

As he gathered his suit jacket, Sarah caught up with him near the door.

"Important call?" she asked, her tone casual but her eyes searching.

"With Fallon," Kareem replied, maintaining eye contact. "Our nightly check-in."

Sarah studied him for a moment, then nodded, something shifting in her expression. "Walk me to the bar first?" she asked, her voice low and warm. "I could use a break from all this acquisition talk. Just five minutes."

Kareem glanced at his watch, hesitating.

"It wont take long," Sarah said. "I think we need to clear the air."

The request was reasonable, and refusing would only make their continued professional interaction more awkward. "Five minutes," he agreed.

They made their way through the restaurant's main dining area, past tables of other business dinners and quiet conversations, until they found a corner of the bar away from the main traffic.

"You've changed," she said softly once their drinks hit the table, eyes lingering on his. "You are... more grounded now."

"People change," Kareem replied.

"Some things don't," Sarah said, her fingers lightly tracing the rim of her glass. "Like the chemistry we had. Still have, if we're being honest."

Kareem didn't deny it, but didn't encourage the observation either. "Sarah—"

"Let me finish," she said, her voice gentle but firm. "I've been putting it out there... little signs, little moments. And you? You've made it clear you're not picking them up. I see that, and I respect it." She took a slow sip of her whiskey, eyes steady. "But I still need to say this—if only so I can stop carrying it around."

She met his eyes directly. "Truth is... part of me just wanted to remind you I was still *that* girl. The one you never really got over. That what we had? It wasn't something you could just replace."

The honesty caught Kareem off guard. "It wasn't about replacement," he said carefully. "What Fallon and I have—it's different. Not better or worse, just... different."

"And now you're fighting for it," Sarah observed.

"Yes."

"I admire that," she said, surprising him. "More than I expected to."

"And part of me? I was running," he said, voice low but firm. "Running from the work, from the hard conversations. When things got rough with Fallon, reaching out to you felt easy—safe. But let me tell you something..." He paused, eyes locked. "Easy ain't always right. And safe? That don't build a life."

Sarah nodded, absorbing this. "Then I hope it works out with her. I mean that."

"Thank you," Kareem said, sensing the genuine goodwill beneath her words.

"And if it doesn't..." She let the sentence hang unfinished, a ghost of possibility rather than an active invitation.

"It was good seeing you again, Sarah," Kareem said, rising from his seat. "But I need to make that call."

She smiled, the expression tinged with resignation and perhaps a touch of newfound respect. "Go. Be where you need to be."

As Kareem made his way out of the restaurant and back toward his hotel, his phone buzzed with Fallon's incoming video call. He answered as he walked, the Chicago street noise forming a backdrop to her image on the screen.

"You're outside," she observed. "Did I catch you at a bad time?"

"No," Kareem replied. "I just stepped out of the team dinner to take your call."

The significance of this choice wasn't lost on Fallon. Her expression softened subtly, and when she spoke, her voice carried a warmth that had been absent in their early calls.

"Tell me about your day," she said.

And as Kareem made his way back to his hotel room, he did just that—sharing not just the facts of the negotiations but his thoughts, his small victories, his frustrations. When he finished, he asked about her weekend, and listened as Fallon described her conversations with her parents, the revelations that had both surprised and clarified things for her.

"My father never fought for my mother," she told him, her voice quiet but steady. "When things became difficult, he chose the easier way out. And somewhere along the way, I realized—that's what I've feared most of my life. Not just being left... but the idea that I might never be worth fighting for at all."

The vulnerability in her admission hung between them, thousands of miles collapsing into the intimate space of shared truth.

"I'm fighting for us," Kareem said simply. "Even when it's hard. Especially when it's hard."

Fallon nodded, her eyes suspiciously bright. "I know. I'm trying to learn how to do the same."

As the call ended, Kareem remained seated on the edge of his hotel bed, a quiet mix of exhaustion and clarity settling over him. Chicago had lived up to its promise—not just as a place to prove his professional worth or his ability to resist old patterns, but as a true test of the marriage he and Fallon were working to rebuild. A marriage rooted not in ease or illusion, but in intention. In choosing connection over convenience, honesty over avoidance. And that, he knew, was the harder path—but the one worth walking. He couldn't know yet if they would succeed. But for the first time in years, he felt they were finally fighting the right battle, together rather than against each other. And that, even in the face of uncertainty, felt like a victory worth cherishing.

Chapter Eleven

Reconstruction

The familiar weight of his house key felt different somehow as Kareem turned it in the lock. Two weeks in Chicago had changed something—not just in his marriage but in himself. He'd gone there fearing temptation and professional pressure; he'd returned with unexpected clarity about what mattered, what he wanted to fight for.

He pushed open the door, rolling his suitcase behind him, and stopped short at the threshold. The living room had been rearranged. The angular armchair was gone, replaced by a small love seat facing two chairs around a low table. A soft throw and warm floor lamp completed the transformation.

"Fallon?" he called, setting down his bags.

She emerged from the kitchen, wiping her hands on a dish towel, dressed casually in jeans and a soft gray sweater—weekend clothes she rarely wore even on weekends.

"Welcome home," she said, her smile tentative but genuine.

"You changed the living room," Kareem observed, still taking in the transformation.

Fallon nodded, a hint of self-consciousness in her posture. “I thought it might be helpful to have a space just for us to talk,” she said thoughtfully. “Somewhere calm, away from the TV and all the little distractions.” She paused, then added with a slight smile, “Dr. Harper calls it a ‘connection corner.’ It sounds a bit... quaint, I know. But the idea felt meaningful.”

The thoughtfulness of the gesture caught Kareem off guard. It wasn’t merely about moving a few things around—it was what the act symbolized. Fallon was making intentional, visible changes, showing in action what words alone could not. She was creating space—not just in the room, but in their relationship—for the healing, for the work, for the partnership they were rebuilding together.

"I like it," he said simply.

Relief flickered across her features. "How was the flight?"

"Flight was delayed." Kareem replied, then added, “But I’m here now. And... I missed you.”

The words emerged more easily than he had expected, without the self-consciousness that might have accompanied them before Chicago. Fallon's eyes widened slightly at the directness, but instead of deflecting or changing the subject, she met his gaze steadily.

"I missed you too," she said warmly. Then, with a graceful smile, "I made dinner—nothing extravagant, just a little pasta. Would you like some?"

"Yes. I’m starving," Kareem said, his tone calm but honest, falling in step behind her. "Lead the way."

As they moved about the kitchen, Kareem noticed a shift—a quiet ease between them, the invisible wall finally softening. At the table, fresh flowers sat in a modest vase. A small gesture, perhaps—but from Fallon, it spoke volumes. She had never been one for unnecessary touches. And yet, here they were.

Fallon glanced over as she picked up her fork, her tone calm and composed. "So, tell me—how does it feel now that everything's official?"

"Good," Kareem replied. "Manley's satisfied with the numbers we landed on. And get this—the CEO of Meridian called me himself this morning. Said he respected how I handled the brand valuation. Told me I brought clarity to a process that's usually all smoke and mirrors."

"That's meaningful," Fallon said, her tone thoughtful, touched with sincere respect. "It's not every day a CEO takes the time to make that kind of call to someone on the team."

"That's what Sarah said too," Kareem commented without thinking, then tensed slightly, unsure how Fallon would react to the casual mention of Sarah's name.

But Fallon simply nodded, taking a sip of her water before asking, "And how did things end with her? Professionally speaking, of course."

"Respectfully," Kareem said, his voice calm but direct. "We talked. Got everything out in the open. By the end of the trip, it was all business—focused, professional. Nothing lingering. Nothing messy."

"Thank you," Fallon said quietly. "For the way you handled it... and for choosing to tell me in the moment, not after the fact."

"I think we're both exhausted—from all the pretending, all the hiding," Kareem said, his tone calm but honest.

Fallon offered a faint, knowing smile, the kind that held more truth than humor. "Well," she replied dryly, "that does sound like something Dr. Harper would say."

They ate in comfortable silence for a moment before Fallon spoke again, her tone deliberately casual but her words carefully chosen.

"We have a therapy session tomorrow at four. Dr. Harper was able to fit us in, even though it's not our regular day. I thought... I thought it might be good to reconnect that way, after your trip."

There was something thoughtful in the way it had all come together—Fallon taking the lead, making the call, choosing to prioritize their healing. It wasn't grand or dramatic, but it didn't need to be. The meaning was in the effort, in the intention behind it. And that, in itself, marked a quiet but significant change.

"That sounds perfect," Kareem agreed.

As they finished dinner, exchanging stories about their two weeks apart, Kareem felt the subtle recalibration of their relationship. There was a shift, a deliberate resetting of the foundation. Not grand gestures, but thoughtful choices, one by one. Each word, each glance, each shared laugh was a brick laid with intention. They were rebuilding—slowly, carefully—something that, this time, just might endure.

Dr. Harper's office felt like familiar territory now, the initial awkwardness of therapeutic space having given way to a sense of purposeful work. She greeted them with her usual calm presence.

"Welcome back, Kareem," she said with a warm smile, peering over her tortoiseshell glasses as she studied him with perceptive eyes. Then she turned to Fallon. "And I understand you've been quite busy during his absence as well."

"I saw my parents," Fallon confirmed, settling into her usual chair. Kareem noticed she no longer brought her portfolio to therapy sessions—another small but significant change. "Separately, as you suggested."

Dr. Harper nodded, removing her glasses and giving Fallon her full attention. "And how was that experience for you?" she asked, allowing a brief silence to follow her question.

"Enlightening," Fallon said with quiet grace. "For the first time, my mother owned her part in the divorce—how her fear of being left made her controlling, and how that very control pushed my father away." She paused, fingers interlaced tightly in her lap. "And my father... he admitted he never truly fought for the marriage. When things got hard, he didn't stay. He just walked away."

"And what did these revelations bring up for you?" Dr. Harper prompted gently, her tone inviting deeper reflection.

"That I've been terrified of both outcomes," Fallon said, her voice steady despite the vulnerability of her words. "Afraid of becoming my mother—so dependent, so desperate for love that I end up pushing Kareem away. And just as afraid of turning into my father—so distant, so emotionally unavailable that I never let anyone close enough to truly know me." She glanced at Kareem, just for a moment. "I've been trying to live somewhere in between, somewhere safe. But I'm starting to understand... that kind of middle ground doesn't really exist."

Dr. Harper leaned forward slightly, her expression compassionate but direct. "Real connection—true, meaningful connection—always comes with risk," she said gently. "The question you have to ask yourself is this: Does the possibility of love, of growth, of something deeper... mean more to you than the fear of being hurt?"

"I think it does," Fallon said quietly.

Kareem felt a surge of emotion at her words—not just what she said, but the undefended way she said it. Without qualifiers, without intellectual distance. Just simple truth.

"Today," Dr. Harper continued, replacing her glasses with that characteristic gesture that signaled she was moving to a new topic, "I'd like to introduce a concept that I think might be helpful as you continue rebuilding your connection: attachment injuries."

"That sounds... medical," Fallon observed, a hint of her professional skepticism surfacing.

Dr. Harper smiled, the expression warm but knowing. "It's actually quite straightforward. An attachment injury happens when someone you depend on doesn't show up in moments when you need them most. Over time, these moments erode the foundation of safety in a relationship."

She took off her glasses slowly, with intention, then looked at each of them—fully, deeply. "You know," she said gently, "these wounds we carry in relations hips... they're rarely the result of someone trying to be cruel. More often, they come from unmet expectations, the way we've learned to communicate—or protect ourselves—long before we ever met the person sitting across from us."

"Like Fallon pulling back," Kareem said, his voice firm but thoughtful

"And just like your tendency to avoid conflict," Dr. Harper added gently but firmly, demonstrating her skill in balanced advocacy. "These patterns—yours and hers—caused wounds. Small ones at first, but over time, they left scars."

Fallon shifted in her chair, discomfort visible on her face. "Are you suggesting that I've caused Kareem trauma?"

"I'm saying you've both created patterns that have wounded each other," Dr. Harper clarified. "But attachment injuries can heal when both partners start responding to vulnerability with empathy rather than defense."

"We been having our daily talks," Kareem said, with a slight nod and a hint of a smile. "Right there in that little 'connection corner' Fallon put together. Her idea. And I gotta admit... it's been good."

Dr. Harper's eyebrows rose slightly, a smile warming her features as she glanced at Fallon. "A connection corner," she repeated, her voice rich and full of encouragement. "Now that... that's a beautiful way to make the idea your own. I love that. Truly."

Fallon looked briefly embarrassed by the praise, but didn't dismiss it as she might have once done. "Well, it just made sense to have a space set aside, something practical."

"It's more than practical," Dr. Harper observed, leaning forward with subtle intensity. "It's symbolic. You're literally making room in your home and your life for emotional connection." She replaced her glasses, the gesture deliberate. "Remember what I've said before—what you permit in your relationship is what will continue. By creating this space, you're permitting connection rather than distance. These are the kinds of changes that rebuild trust—consistent small actions that demonstrate commitment to new patterns."

Her words carried the quiet strength of a woman who had lived, learned, and refused to be undone by either. There was a calm certainty in her voice, the kind that only comes from lessons earned the hard way. And as Kareem listened, he couldn't help but wonder—what had she walked through to speak of healing with such clarity and grace?

"Now, let's talk about how these attachment injuries manifest in your marriage," Dr. Harper continued. "Fallon, what you were doing—that emotional distance—that was your way of protecting yourself, and I see that. I truly do. But for Kareem? It didn't feel like protection. It felt like abandonment. Especially in the moments when he was reaching out, needing closeness, needing you."

She turned to Kareem, her gaze equally direct. "And Kareem, withdrawing from conflict doesn't make it disappear. What it does is leave room for silence to grow, for questions to go unanswered. And for Fallon, that silence likely felt like neglect. Like the very thing she feared most—that the love, the effort, the vulnerability—was one-sided."

The precision of her observations hit both of them with uncomfortable accuracy. She had named what had remained unnamed between them for so long, translating their patterns into terms they could finally understand.

"True intimacy requires both of you to be vulnerable, even when it's uncomfortable," Dr. Harper said, her voice softening. "It means learning to recognize when old patterns are being triggered and making different choices in those moments."

She let the silence stretch for a moment, giving them time to absorb this before continuing. "Many couples fall into a cycle where one partner feels undervalued or misunderstood, so they withdraw, causing the other partner to either pursue harder or give up entirely. Breaking this cycle starts with recognizing it's happening."

Throughout the session, Dr. Harper guided them through examples of attachment injuries in their relationship—moments when each had needed the other and found emptiness instead. She didn't hurry them past the hard truths. She let the discomfort settle, understanding that real growth often begins in the places we'd rather not linger.

"For next week," Dr. Harper said as they concluded, replacing her glasses once more, "I'd like you to practice noticing when these attachment patterns are triggered. When Fallon feels the urge to withdraw emotionally, or when Kareem feels the impulse to avoid conflict. Just notice it. No blame, no judgment. And if you feel ready... share that moment with each other. Because healing begins with noticing—and connection begins with truth."

She leaned forward, her expression serious but encouraging. "Remember, rebuilding trust happens in the little things—every honest word, every moment you choose to show up. A marriage is like a garden. You can't just show up when it's dying. You have to tend it daily. Water it. Nurture it. That's how love grows."

The metaphor landed with quiet force, its simple truth impossible to dismiss. Kareem looked over at Fallon, and in her eyes, he saw it—the same realization taking root. What they were rebuilding wasn't about grand gestures or sudden change. It was going to take time. Patience. Steady, intentional effort. The kind of care that goes deep. The kind that transforms.

As they walked side by side to the parking garage, the weight of that truth stayed with Kareem. Their relationship hadn't unraveled in a single moment. It had worn down over years, through a thousand small silences, missed opportunities, and unmet needs—each one a quiet crack in their foundation. And if they were going to make it, really make it, they'd have to do the work. With care. With consistency. With love that shows up even when it's hard. Because healing—true healing—isn't loud. But it changes everything.

"That was intense," he commented as they reached their car. "That hit deeper than I expected."

"Yes," Fallon agreed, her expression thoughtful. "But necessary." She met his eyes across the top of the car, steady and sincere. "I never really thought of it as trauma before—how my emotional distance might have hurt you."

"And I never realized how my conflict avoidance enabled the pattern," Kareem admitted. "I thought I was being patient, but I was actually making it worse."

They drove home wrapped in a thoughtful silence, the kind that sinks in deep when truth has been spoken. Dr. Harper's words lingered, gently echoing in their minds: healing isn't grand or dramatic—it's built in the small, consistent choices we make every day. A relationship, she'd said, is like a garden. It needs tending, watering, sunlight—not just frantic care when the leaves start to wilt. That lesson—quiet but powerful—was settling in.

The text came on Wednesday afternoon, just a single line from Fallon: *Lost the Henderson case. Judgment for the defendant.*

Kareem stared down at his phone, and in that moment, he knew exactly what it meant. The Henderson case wasn't just another file on Fallon's desk—it had been the heartbeat of her professional life for months. A tangled web of corporate liability, high stakes, and even higher expectations. Losing it wasn't just a loss in court—it was a crack in the image she'd so carefully built. The image of the woman who always had the answers, always won, always rose above. And when that kind of identity takes a hit... it shakes you to your core.

He called immediately, unsure if she would answer. To his surprise, she picked up on the second ring.

"Are you okay?" he asked without preamble.

A long pause, then Fallon's voice, smaller than he had ever heard it: "No. Not really."

The admission itself was remarkable—a departure from her usual insistence on being fine, having everything under control. Kareem caught himself, took a breath, and remembered what Dr. Harper had said. That men often want to jump in and fix, to solve—but sometimes, what a woman really needs is to be heard. To be understood. Not solved. So instead of rushing in, he listened. He stayed present.

"Do you want to talk about it?" he asked, consciously pushing aside his instinct to immediately offer solutions.

"Not yet," Fallon replied. "I just... I don't want to be alone right now. Could you come home early?"

The vulnerability in the request tightened something in Kareem's chest. "Of course. I'll be there in half an hour."

He found her in the connection corner, curled into the love seat, still in her court clothes but with her shoes kicked off. She looked up as he entered, her eyes red-rimmed but dry.

"That was fast," she observed.

"Traffic wasn't bad,"Kareem said, settling into one of the chairs across from her. "What do you need right now?"

The question itself was simple—remarkably so. But in its simplicity, it held a quiet kind of power. It didn't assume. It didn't push. It simply asked. A gesture of presence, not pressure. And for a moment, Fallon looked almost startled by it, as if the notion of someone truly asking what she needed—rather than deciding for her—was unfamiliar territory.

"Just... this," she said finally. "Someone to sit with while I process. I'm not ready to dissect what went wrong or strategize about appeals. I just need to feel the disappointment before I start problem-solving."

Kareem nodded, this time with understanding rather than urgency. Once upon a time, he would've leapt into problem-solving mode—offering solutions when what she truly needed was to be heard.And Fallon? She would've done what she always did—pulled that professional mask into place, claimed she was "fine," and buried the ache beneath polished composure. It was her armor. But that armor, as strong as it was, had kept out more than just pain. It had kept out connection too.

So instead, they sat together—side by side—in the stillness of their living room, the soft light casting gentle patterns across the floor. Kareem didn't speak just to fill the silence. He didn't try to fix, to smooth over, or explain away her pain. He simply stayed. Fully present. Quietly attentive. And in that moment, his presence was more meaningful than any words could've been—a quiet affirmation that she didn't have to carry her disappointment alone.

Eventually, Fallon began to talk—about the case, the judge's reasoning, the moments in court when she realized things were turning against her. Kareem listened, asking occasional questions but mostly allowing her to process aloud without interruption or judgment.

"The worst part," she admitted finally, "is feeling like I failed. I built my identity around being exceptional, never losing, always finding the angle. And today... I lost. Not privately, not quietly, but in full view. And there's no spinning it."

"You didn't fail," Kareem said quietly. "You lost a case. There's a difference."

"Is there?" Fallon asked, genuine uncertainty in her voice.

"Failure would be not preparing, not giving your best effort, not caring about the outcome," Kareem observed. "You did everything possible. Sometimes the result is beyond our control."

Fallon absorbed this, her expression thoughtful. "When did you get so wise?" she asked, a small smile finally breaking through.

"I've had some good conversations lately," Kareem replied, returning her smile. "With a very insightful woman."

"Dr. Harper is pretty perceptive," Fallon agreed.

"I wasn't talking about Dr. Harper," Kareem said quietly.

The moment hung between them, the compliment landing with unexpected weight. Fallon's eyes met his, surprise giving way to something warmer, more vulnerable.

"Thank you," she said simply. "For coming home. For sitting with me. For... seeing me, even when I'm not at my best."

"Especially then," Kareem replied.

The Jefferson Square block party had always been a tradition—one of those warm, familiar gatherings where everyone brought a dish, the kids ran free on the lawn, and neighbors, after months of passing waves and hurried hellos, finally slowed down to reconnect. Unlike previous years when they'd attended out of obligation, tonight felt different as Kareem and Fallon navigated the crowded room. Her hand rested lightly on his arm as they moved through the space—a small but visible sign of connection that hadn't been present before.

They had just joined a conversation about the neighborhood's planned tree-planting initiative when Kareem spotted Devon and Vanessa entering, Devon's boisterous greeting to the host drawing attention as always.

"Devon and Vanessa are here," he murmured to Fallon.

She followed his gaze, her expression revealing nothing. "We should say hello," she said. "But not just yet. Let's get something to eat first."

They filled plates and joined the Harrises and a young couple new to the neighborhood. The conversation flowed easily until Dave Harris turned to Kareem.

“You’re in finance, right? So tell me—what’s your take on all this noise about interest rates?”

"They're concerning," Kareem began, launching into an analysis of potential market impacts when Devon's voice boomed behind him.

"Listen to my man, dropping knowledge!" Devon settled into an empty chair, Vanessa following with noticeably less enthusiasm. "There he goes—our forever voice of reason, Mr. Kareem himself."

And just like clockwork, the familiar pattern emerged—Devon’s signature brand of praise, laced ever so gently with just enough condescension to make it sting. Always finding a way to reassert himself as the one in control, the alpha in the room. Kareem recognized the shift and steadied himself, already knowing the next move was coming.

What he hadn’t anticipated—what truly caught him off guard—was Fallon’s intervention.

"Kareem's insight is why Ellis & Dean just put him in charge of the Meridian acquisition," she said, her voice carrying the precise combination of casual confidence and pride that commanded attention. "He negotiated terms that had their CEO personally calling to express appreciation."

The energy at the table shifted—what had begun as polite conversation turned into real, engaged curiosity. All eyes were on Kareem now, and for good reason. He spoke with clarity, confidence, and purpose. What he noticed most, though, was Fallon. She sat beside him, no longer the commanding presence at the center of it all, but intentionally quiet—supportive. She asked no questions, offered no corrections. Instead, she made room for him to lead, to shine, in a space where she had once held the spotlight. And that, in its own way, spoke volumes.

As the conversation unfolded, Kareem caught Devon watching, his expression caught somewhere between curiosity and quiet confusion.

Later, as Kareem returned from the bar, Devon intercepted him. "Let me talk to you for a second," he said, nodding toward the hallway.

"Something's different," he observed, studying Kareem with unusual intensity. "You and Fallon... y'all moving different. I ain't never seen her look at you like that before."

"We're working on things," Kareem replied neutrally.

"Nah, man... it's more than that," Devon shook his head slowly. "Maybe you was right to try, man. Maybe you've been right the whole time. But don't let that go to your head, you hear me?"

The admission caught Kareem off guard—not just the words themselves, but the hint of something like regret beneath them.

"Nah... it hasn't been easy," Kareem said carefully.

"Ain't nothing worth having ever easy," Devon replied, his voice carrying unexpected longing. Before he could say more, Vanessa appeared.

"There you are," she said, her tone overly bright. "The Mitchells need those Cabo details."

The moment dissolved, Devon's reflective mood replaced by his usual social persona as he rejoined his wife. But something had been revealed in that brief exchange—a crack in Devon's carefully maintained facade, a glimpse of questioning beneath his certainty.

One week later, they hosted a quiet dinner with two couples from work—nothing extravagant, just good food, good wine, and the kind of easy conversation that slowly peels back the layers of professionalism. The evening had gone beautifully. Now, with the guests gone and the house settling into its evening hush, Kareem felt a calm kind of joy in the simple rhythm of cleaning up beside Fallon. She rinsed the dishes, he loaded the dishwasher, their movements flowing in harmony. This was partnership.

"That was nice," Fallon observed, handing him a serving platter. "The Taylors have such warm energy—genuinely good company."

"They are," Kareem agreed. "And you were right about Jim. He's funnier than he lets on. Caught me off guard a couple times."

"I told you," Fallon said with a small smile. "I appreciated the way you encouraged Andrea to talk about her photography. She rarely opens up like that at work"

"Everybody's got layers, things they don't show when they're on the clock," Kareem said, locking eyes with her. "Even you."

"Especially me," Fallon acknowledged, the self-awareness in her tone a marker of how far they had come.

As they turned out the kitchen lights and headed upstairs, Fallon paused, turning to face him with an expression of quiet determination.

"I need to tell you something," she said, her voice soft but clear.

"What is it?" Kareem asked, suddenly alert to the seriousness in her tone.

"I'm proud of you," Fallon said, her voice steady, clear. "Not just for what you've accomplished in your career—though that matters, and I am proud of that too. But I'm proud of the man you are. The integrity you carry, the patience you've shown, and the strength it took to lean in and do the hard work of healing us... when walking away would've been so much easier." She paused, took a breath, and met his eyes without flinching. "And I'm sorry—for the times I didn't see you, didn't honor you, didn't make room for the fullness of who you are."

Kareem felt the weight of her words, their sincerity, their healing potential.

"Thank you," he said, reaching for her hand.

As they climbed the stairs together, hand in hand, Kareem felt the subtle but profound shift in their marriage—less a dramatic transformation than a careful reconstruction. It was crafted piece by piece from fresh understanding, purposeful decisions to reach out instead of pulling back, choosing to truly see each other rather than turning away, and committing to stay present instead of slipping into avoidance.

Chapter Twelve

Renewed Vows

As the sun stretched its golden fingers across the kitchen floor, Kareem stood at the counter, brewing coffee the way he always had. But this morning felt… different. Not because the routine had changed, but because *he* had. It had been six months since their marriage stood on the edge of something neither of them wanted to name. And yet, here they were—still standing. As he spooned out the coffee grounds with quiet intention, his eyes wandered to the signs of their slow healing: Fallon's favorite mug nestled beside his own, a calendar now peppered with both their handwriting, and photos—yes, real, honest snapshots—tacked to the fridge. Nothing posed. Nothing perfect. Just the beautiful, messy evidence of two people choosing, every day, to stay in it together.

Fallon appeared in the doorway, already dressed in her running clothes. "Morning," she said, moving to the refrigerator for water. "Did you sleep well?"

"Pretty good," Kareem replied, pouring her a cup of coffee before she asked—a small gesture of attentiveness they'd both learned to practice. "But I'll be honest with you," he added, looking up with that familiar weight behind his eyes. "I was up thinking about the ceremony. Kept checking that forecast like I could change the clouds myself."

"It's just a little rain predicted," Fallon said, accepting the coffee with a grateful nod. "And honestly? Maybe that's fitting. Marriage isn't just about perfect sunny days."

Kareem studied her face, quietly struck by the transformation he witnessed. This was not the guarded, tightly-wound woman who once measured herself against every unexpected forecast. The Fallon of a year ago would've unraveled at the hint of rain—seeing it not as nature's whim, but as some reflection of personal failure. But now she met uncertainty with grace, as if she'd finally made peace with the truth: some things simply aren't meant to be controlled.

"Two o'clock with Dr. Harper?" she asked, checking her watch.

"Yeah... last one-on-one before the big show. Gotta make it count."

Fallon nodded, understanding the significance. "I'm having lunch with Jessica at noon. I just... felt it was important to check in with her too."

"You tell her I said hello," Kareem said, then added with a hint of his dry humor, "And tell her thank you... for not giving up on us."

Fallon smiled, the expression reaching her eyes in a way that once would have been rare. "I'll make sure to tell her." She paused at the doorway. "Kareem? Be honest. Are you nervous about tomorrow?"

He considered the question with the honesty they'd worked so hard to cultivate. "I wouldn't say nervous. It's... respect. Reverence. Like we're acknowledging something sacred that we almost lost."

"That's a good word for it," she agreed softly. "Reverence."

She stepped closer and gently brushed her lips against his cheek—a gesture that once seemed as unfamiliar as foreign soil but now felt as natural as breathing—and headed out for her morning run. Kareem stood there, coffee mug cradled in his hands, watching her leave with the kind of quiet satisfaction that settles deep in your bones when gratitude takes up permanent residence.

Alone in the house after Fallon left, Kareem found himself drawn to his home office, where a small framed photo sat on the desk. It was from his financial firm's awards dinner last month—not a couple's photo, just him accepting recognition for the Meridian acquisition.

He picked it up, letting his eyes linger on the image. The man in that photo... he stood taller. His smile reached his eyes. There was a lightness in his expression, an ease that hadn't been there a year ago. And that's when Kareem realized—this wasn't just about his marriage finding its way back to center. This was something deeper. He was seeing himself clearly, maybe for the first time in years. Not Fallon's husband. Not the reliable one at the office. Just

Kareem—whole, worthy, and quietly powerful in his own right. What he'd built within himself wasn't dependent on anyone else. It was his. And it would remain his, no matter what came next.

In the quiet of reflection, Kareem had come to understand something essential—something it had taken years to unravel. His value was never meant to be measured by how well he smoothed things over, or how often he kept the peace at the expense of his own voice. No, his worth wasn't rooted in pleasing everyone or sidestepping discomfort. It came from a deeper place. From integrity. From emotional honesty. From the quiet courage it takes to stand in your truth—even when it trembles—while still holding space for the truths of others. These weren't new traits. They'd always been there, tucked beneath years of shouldering expectations and playing it safe. All they'd ever needed was permission. And now, at last, they had it.

Setting the photo down, Kareem felt a quiet certainty settle over him. Whatever tomorrow brought—whatever the years ahead held—he was anchored now in something unshakeable.

Dr. Harper's office was exactly as it had always been—calm, orderly, intentionally understated. But what had changed, profoundly, was the man seated across from her now.

"Our final indiviual session," she said, peering over her glasses. "How are you feeling about tomorrow?"

"Feels big," Kareem admitted.

"How are you feeling about tomorrow?"

Kareem considered this, taking his time—another change from the man who once rushed to please with quick, acceptable answers.

"Grateful," he said finally. "But also... humbled. When I think about how close I came to throwing everything away..."

Dr. Harper nodded, neither dismissing his regret nor allowing him to dwell in it. "That choice you made with Sarah," she said gently, "showed who you really are."

"I still think about it sometimes," Kareem admitted.

"Regret can be a teacher," Dr. Harper observed. "It shows us we can fall and still rise." She removed her glasses, a signal she was shifting to a deeper level of conversation. "So let me ask you this—from where you sit now, looking at your marriage... what do you see that your heart couldn't recognize six months ago?"

Kareem leaned back, truly considering the question. "You know... what I see now is space," he said, nodding slightly. "Not that cold, silent distance we used to live in—but real space. Space to breathe. To speak. To be. Room for her to be her. For me to be me. Room to disagree and not think the whole thing is going to fall apart.

Dr. Harper smiled, approval warming her expression. "That's beautifully said."

"I've learned that marriage isn't about finding your 'better half,'" Kareem continued, his voice carrying the weight of hard-earned truth. He gave a small nod, remembering. "You said that once... months ago. I didn't really hear it then. But now? Now I get it."

He looked up, meeting Dr. Harper's gaze.

"It's two whole people—flawed, growing, still figuring it out—making the choice. Every day. To show up. To build something that doesn't erase who you are...

but honors it. Strengthens it." He paused, the words settling between them. "That's the kind of marriage I want. Not perfect. Just real."

"And Fallon? How would you describe her journey?" Dr Harper questioned.

"She's... braver than I ever gave her credit for," Kareem said, his voice softening with admiration. ""Those walls? They were protection. Fear built them." He paused, eyes narrowing just a bit. "But letting them down... even a little? That takes real strength. The kind most people never find."

"And your journey?"

"I don't hide anymore. Not from conflict, not from what I need, not from the truth. I used to think keeping the peace was the same as building connection. It's not."

Dr. Harper replaced her glasses, signaling a shift toward practical matters. "What tools do you feel have been most valuable?"

"Our daily check-ins." Kareem said, steady and sure. "They've been a game-changer. Just fifteen minutes—no distractions, no talk about who's picking up what or what bills are due. Just... truth. Feelings. Fears. What we're hoping for. At first, it felt like nothing. But now? It's changed everything."

"Small consistent actions over time," Dr. Harper nodded. "The garden metaphor."

"Exactly. And learning to recognize our patterns—when Fallon starts to withdraw or when I start avoiding. Being able to see it, call it out, right then—not after the damage is done? Man... that's been everything.

Dr. Harper studied him with the measured gaze that had become so familiar—assessing, caring, perceptive.

"Marriage is never finished," she said. "It's how you choose to meet challenges together that matters."

"I know our marriage isn't perfect," Kareem acknowledged. "But it has something now that it didn't have before."

"And what's that?"

"Foundation," he said simply. "Real foundation. Not shared bills or a couch you both picked out. But trust that's been tested. Communication that's survived silence. Love that chose to stay even when it would have been easier to go."

As their session drew to a close, she leaned forward slightly. "Just remember—recommitment isn't only about honoring the progress you've made. It's about recognizing that the journey is still unfolding. And it continues with intention, with mindfulness, and above all, with the power of choice."

Kareem nodded, absorbing her words. "Thank you," he said simply. "For everything."

"The work was yours," Dr. Harper replied, her quiet dignity filling the room. "I just created the space for it to happen."

As he stood to leave, Kareem paused. "Can I ask you something personal?"

Dr. Harper's eyebrow lifted slightly, but she nodded.

"What made you choose this work? Helping couples rebuild when it would be easier to walk away?"

A shadow passed briefly across her face, quickly replaced by the composed expression he knew well. “Maybe,” she said gently, “because I've come to understand that the easiest path isn't always the one that brings real healing. And sometimes," she paused, her voice rich with knowing, "the things that break us... can be put back together. Stronger. Wiser. Right at the seams."

It wasn't a complete answer, but in its careful boundaries, Kareem recognized something familiar—the wisdom of knowing which parts of ourselves to share and which to hold sacred.

The restaurant buzzed with lunchtime energy as Fallon settled across from Jessica, who was already halfway through her iced tea.

"You look different," Jessica observed. "More... here. Like you're actually in your life instead of watching it happen."

The observation landed with unexpected weight. Once, Fallon might have deflected such personal insight with a polished laugh or swift subject change. Now, she simply nodded, accepting the truth in her friend's words.

"That's... actually exactly how it feels," she admitted. "Like I've stepped into my own life instead of directing it from offstage."

"The ceremony tomorrow—you nervous?"

Fallon smiled. "Not in the way you'd think. It's not about getting the details perfect this time."

"Unlike your actual wedding," Jessica laughed. "Girl, I *still* remember you losing sleep over finding the perfect shade of blue for those table runners."

"God, I was impossible," Fallon groaned. "All that energy spent on appearances, and I completely missed the point."

"Which was?"

"The wedding is just a day. The marriage is the journey." She traced her water glass. "And I realized something about my parents."

"What's that?"

"That I've been punishing Kareem for their mistakes. Making him pay for damage he didn't cause."

Jessica nodded slowly. "Okay... that was actually deep."

"Don't sound so shocked," Fallon said dryly.

"I'm not surprised you figured it out," Jessica said with a playful smirk. "I'm surprised you actually said it out loud."

As they finished, Jessica reached across the table and squeezed Fallon's hand. “I'm proud of you,” she said, her voice soft but steady. “What you and Kareem are doing—choosing to stay, to fight for each other instead of just calling it quits—that's real courage, girl.”

Fallon felt unexpected emotion tighten her throat. “Thank you... for not giving up on me. Even when I wasn't the easiest to love.”

"Please," Jessica scoffed, lightening the moment. “If I gave up on difficult people, I'd be sitting at brunch by myself. Especially with all the lawyers I know.”

The coffee shop buzzed with mid-afternoon energy as Kareem slid into the booth across from Devon. His friend looked up from his phone, that familiar charismatic smile spreading across his face, though something about it seemed different—muted, perhaps, or simply more authentic.

"My man," Devon said, extending his hand for their usual greeting. "The groom himself—Mr. Big Time! Looking' like he just walked off a magazine cover!"

"Not technically a groom this time around," Kareem pointed out, accepting the coffee Devon had already ordered for him—black, no sugar, just as he preferred.

“Man, I don’t care what you call it—round two at the altar? That’s something serious!

There was a brief silence, neither uncomfortable nor easy—the kind that exists between men who've known each other too long for pretense but are navigating new territory in their friendship.

"Thanks for meeting me," Kareem said finally. "Means a lot that you're coming tomorrow."

Devon shrugged, but the casualness seemed practiced. "Man, please—I wasn’t gonna miss it. Plus, Vanessa been yapping’ about it all week. Talkin’ about, ‘Ooo it’s romantic!’ I’m just trying’ to keep the peace!”

"And you?"

"Me?" Devon's eyebrow arched. "Since when do you care what I think about romance?"

"Since always," Kareem replied honestly. "You've been the one I bounce things off of—through all of this. Even when we didn't see eye to eye."

Devon's expression shifted, the practiced nonchalance giving way to something more vulnerable. "Yeah, well." He turned his coffee cup slowly. "Maybe I ain't always been the best one to be giving advice, alright?

"What do you mean?"

Devon met his eyes directly—unusual for a man who typically maintained casual eye contact, never allowing a gaze to linger long enough for real connection.

"I took the easy way out," he said, voice low. "Didn't try to fix nothing with Vanessa. Just found... other options. Like a coward."

The admission hung between them, its weight significant.

"It's not too late," Kareem said quietly.

Devon's laugh held little humor. "Easy to say when you the one that actually did the work!"

"The work is still there if you want it."

Devon nodded slowly, absorbing this. "Maybe. Been thinking about it. Watching you and Fallon—how different y'all are now." He shook his head. "Make a man sit back and say, 'maybe it ain't too late after all.'"

"It wasn't easy," Kareem said. "Still isn't."

"Boy, didn't I tell you? Ain't nothing worth havin' ever come easy. I swear you don't listen."Devon replied, echoing their conversation from months earlier, but this time with genuine reflection rather than glib certainty.

As they prepared to leave, Devon hesitated. "You really think it's possible, man? To change stuff that's been sitting in you that deep?"

"I do," Kareem said without hesitation. "But you have to be willing to see yourself clearly first. That's the hardest part."

Devon nodded, absorbing this. "Look here, man—I'm happy for you. Dead serious. What you got with Fallon? That's real, man. That ain't that play-play mess—y'all got the kind of love folks be out here praying for, but too scared to work for."

As they parted outside, Devon's handshake lingered a moment longer than usual. "See you tomorrow," he said, then added with unexpected sincerity, "I'm proud of you, man. Real talk."

Morning sun glittered across the water as Kareem and Fallon walked barefoot along the beach where they'd first met thirteen years earlier. No elaborate decorations, no audience—just the two of them, the sound of waves, and the promises they were about to remake with clearer understanding of their weight.

They stopped at the spot they'd chosen, a small cove sheltered by driftwood, and turned to face each other. Fallon wore a simple ivory dress that moved with the breeze, while Kareem had chosen a lightweight linen shirt and pants, rolled at the ankles. Their formality had been replaced by something more essential—presence, intention, truth.

"I'd like to go first," Fallon said, her voice steady as she unfolded a small piece of paper. "If that's okay."

Kareem nodded, watching as she took a deep breath.

"Kareem," she began, her voice steady and thoughtful, "years ago, I stood beside you and made vows I didn't fully comprehend. I promised you forever, not yet realizing the depth of what that truly meant—the effort it would take, the strength it would call for, and the way it would ask both of us to grow, again and again."

The breeze caught at her as she continued, her eyes never leaving his.

"I built walls, thinking they would keep me safe—never realizing they were also shutting out the very love I needed. I tested your devotion when I should have trusted it. And I held pieces of myself back, convincing myself that distance was the same as protection. It wasn't."

Her voice grew stronger, more certain with each word.

"Today, I make new vows—with eyes wide open and a heart willing to do the work. I promise to choose courage when fear tries to take the lead. To risk being vulnerable, rather than hide behind the mask of perfection. To see you—really see you—not as a reflection of what I imagined, but as the person you are."

She paused, her voice catching for just a moment before steadying again.

"I promise to stand with you, not in opposition. To remember that our differences aren't barriers, but the threads that strengthen the fabric of what we're building. And most of all, I promise to believe in a love that doesn't run from the storm—but holds firm until the skies clear."

She folded the paper, tucking it away. "I choose you, Kareem. Not because I need you to complete me, but because together, we create something greater than either of us alone."

The emotion in Kareem's eyes matched her own as he drew out his own folded paper.

"Fallon," he said, his voice calm but firm, eyes locked on hers. "When we met, I thought I had love all figured out. Thought it was about the big moments—the flowers, the fireworks, the picture-perfect scenes. But I was wrong. Real love... real love shows up in the quiet. In the hard talks. In the staying, even when walking away would be easier. It's choosing each other—not once, but every single day."

The sunlight caught the moisture in his eyes, but his gaze remained unwavering.

"I let things slide that I shouldn't have. I chose keeping the peace over speaking the truth. I stayed quiet when I should've spoken up. And in that silence... resentment grew—right where honesty should've lived."

He took a step closer, his free hand finding hers.

"Today," he began, steady and clear, "I make a vow—to speak my truth, but with grace. To stand in who I am, without stepping on who you are. To see those old habits when they try to creep in... and choose better."

He paused, his voice dropping with quiet conviction.

"I promise you patience—but not the kind that stays silent when it matters. Strength—not to control, but to uplift. And love... not in spite of our flaws, but because we're willing to face them together."

He folded the paper and slipped it into his pocket. "I choose you, Fallon. Not some perfect picture I had in my head. I'm talking about *you*—the real woman, layered, complicated, extraordinary. I choose us. Just like this. Growing. Becoming who we're supposed to be... together."

They exchanged simple bands, symbols of this new chapter written with wiser hearts.

As they sealed their vows with a kiss, the first light raindrops began to fall—gentle, cleansing, perfect in their imperfection. They laughed, neither moving to seek shelter, allowing the rain to touch them as they held each other close.

Later, as they walked along the shoreline at sunset, Fallon paused. She looked at Kareem—really looked at him—then smiled, stepping closer to take his hand. A year ago, even this simple gesture would have felt unfamiliar. But now it was natural—the freedom, the ease, the love they'd rediscovered. Their shadows stretched across the wet sand—two distinct figures, yes, but moving in step, becoming one in the soft glow of the fading light.

In that quiet moment, the truth of their journey came into focus—not as some dramatic breakthrough, but as something more meaningful: the choice to be present, together.

Their marriage wasn't suddenly perfect. It was alive—growing, requiring daily care. As they made their way back across the beach, Fallon leaned against his shoulder. "What now?" she asked softly.

"Now?" Kareem replied, his voice warm with certainty. "We keep choosing each other. Every single day. When it's easy, yeah—but especially when it's not."

In the stillness of the night, they held each other close—understanding, at last, that love is not defined by the absence of storms, but by the decision to face them side by side. And in that choice, steady and intentional, like seeds nurtured with care and patience, something strong and beautiful would continue to grow.

www.ingramcontent.com/pod-product-compliance
Lightning Source LLC
LaVergne TN
LVHW100518110826
845146LV00002B/688

* 9 7 9 8 9 9 9 2 6 8 2 1 1 *